THE BOBBSEY TWINS BOOKS
By Laura Lee Hope

"Shall we go up inside?" Nan asked.

The Bobbsey Twins in Washington

The Bobbsey Twins in Washington

By

LAURA LEE HOPE

GROSSET & DUNLAP
Publishers   New York

———

THE BOBBSEY TWINS IN WASHINGTON

CONTENTS

CHAPTER I

UNDER THE HAY

"This is 'most as much fun as we had on Blueberry Island, or when we went to Florida on the deep, blue sea, isn't it, Bert?" asked Nan Bobbsey, as she sat on the porch and fanned herself with her hat. She and her brother had been running around the house, playing a new game, and Nan was warm.

"Yes, it's fun all right," agreed Bert. "But I liked the deep, blue sea better—or even Blueberry Island," and off came his hat to cool his flushed face, for, though it was late in September, the day was warm.

"But we couldn't stay on the island, always," went on Nan. "We have to go to school, daddy says!"

"Don't speak about it!" begged Bert. "I don't want to go to school for a long, long time, and not then!"

"Have we got to go to school?" asked a little light-haired and blue-eyed girl, as she ran up the steps, to sink in a heap at the feet of her sister, Nan Bobbsey. "When do we go?" she went on.

"Oh, not right away, 'little fat fairy!'" laughed Nan, giving Flossie the name her father sometimes called her. "School won't open for two weeks more."

"Hurray!" cried Bert. "The longer it stays closed the better I like it. But come on, Nan! Let's have some more fun. This isn't like Blueberry Island, sitting still on a porch!"

"You haven't sat still more than three minutes, Bert Bobbsey!" cried his sister. "I can hardly get my breath, you made me run so fast!"

Just then a little boy, who had the same sort of blue eyes and golden hair that made Flossie such a pretty little girl, came tumbling up the steps with a clatter and a bang, falling down at Bert's feet. The older boy caught his small brother just in time, or there might have been a bumped nose.

"Hi there, Freddie, what's the matter?" asked Bert, with a laugh. "Is our dog Snap chasing you, or have you been playing a trick on our cat Snoop?"

"I—I—I'm a—a fireman!" panted Freddie. for he, too, was out of breath from running. "I'm a fireman, and I—I've got to get the engine. There's a big, big fire!" and his eyes opened wide and round.

"A big fire—really?" asked Nan quickly.

"Course not! He's only making believe!" replied Bert.

"Well, I thought maybe he might have seen some boys start a bonfire somewhere," explained Nan. "They sometimes do."

"I know they do," admitted Bert. "And I hope they don't start one near daddy's lumberyard."

"There was a fire down in the lumber once!" exclaimed Freddie. He was too young to have seen it, but he had heard his father and mother talk about the time Mr. Bobbsey's lumberyard was nearly burned out. Freddie

Bobbsey was very fond of a toy fire engine he had been given for Christmas, and his father often called Freddie a "little fireman," just as Flossie was named a "fairy."

"Well, if it's only a make-believe fire we can sit here and cool off," went on Nan. "What were you doing, Flossie?" she asked her little sister.

"Oh, I was having a race with our cat Snoop; but I guess I beat, 'cause Snoop didn't get here to the porch before I did."

"Yes, you won the race all right," laughed Bert. "But it's too hot for any more running games. I wish we were back on the island where we found that boy, Jack Nelson, and could play we were sailors and could splash in the water."

"That would be fun!" sighed Nan, as she fanned herself harder than ever with her hat.

The Bobbsey twins had, a few days before, returned to their home from a vacation spent on a strange island off the coast of Florida. They had gone there with Cousin Jasper Dent to rescue a boy who had been left in a lonely cave, and very many strange adventures the

Bobbsey twins and their father and mother, to say nothing of Cousin Jasper, had had on that voyage.

Now the simple games they tried to get up around the house, and the thought of having to go back to school soon, made them feel a bit lonesome for the deep, blue sea, over which they had made a voyage to rescue the boy, Jack Nelson, and also for Blueberry Island, where once they spent a vacation.

"I know what we can do!" cried Nan, after a rest.

"What?" asked Bert, always ready to join Nan in any fun she thought of. "What can we do?"

"Go out to the barn and play that's a ship like the one we went on to Florida. It'll be cooler in the barn than it is here, anyhow."

"That's so," admitted Bert. "And oh! I know how we can have packs of fun!"

"How?" This time it was Nan who eagerly asked.

"Why we can swing on some of the ropes that are in the haymow I guess the ropes are there to tie things up on in the winter. But we can swing on 'em now, and make believe we're sailors, just as we did when we found that boy in the cave where we went with Cousin Jasper."

"Oh, so we can!" cried Nan. "Come on!"

"I'll be a fireman on the ship!" declared fat Freddie, as he got slowly to his feet from the floor where he had been sitting near Bert. I'll be a fireman and squirt water."

"Not real—only make believe" cried Bert. "Water spoils hay, you know, Freddie. You can't splash any water on daddy's hay in the barn."

"No, I'll only make believe," agreed the light-haired little boy. "Come on Flossie!" he called to his sister, who had slipped down off the porch to run after a big black cat that marched along with his tail in the air, "like a fishing pole," Bert said. "Come on, Flossie!" called Freddie. "We'll go out to the barn and play ship and sailors, and I'll be a fireman and you can be——"

"I'm going to be hungry, and have something good to eat! That's what I'll be," declared Flossie quickly. "I'm going to be *awful* hungry!"

"Oh dear!" exclaimed Nan, but she was laughing. "That's always the way. Those two want to do something different."

"Well, we can all make believe we're hungry," said Bert. "And maybe Dinah will give us some cookies to eat."

"There she goes now. I'll ask her!" offered Nan, as she saw the Bobbsey's fat and good-natured colored cook cross the lawn with a small basket of clothes to hang up. "We'll have a little play-party out in the barn."

"But I'm going to be real hungry—not make believe!" said Freddie. "I want to eat real."

"And so you can!" declared Nan. "I'll get enough for all of us."

A little later the Bobbsey twins—the two pairs of them—were on the way to the barn that stood a little way back of the house. Mr. Bobbsey did not live on a farm. He lived in a town, but his place was large enough to have a barn on it as well as a house. He kept a horse, and sometimes a cow, but just now there was no cow in the stable—only a horse.

And the horse was not there, either, just then, for it was being used to pull a wagon about the streets of Lakeport. Mr. Bobbsey had an automobile, but he also kept the horse, and this animal was sometimes used by the clerks from the lumber office.

So out to the barn, which had in it the winter supply of hay and oats for the horse, went the Bobbsey twins. Nan and Bert, being older, reached the place first, each one carrying some sugar and molasses cookies Dinah had given them. After Nan and Bert ran Flossie and Freddie, each one looking anxiously at the packages of cookies.

"Don't those cookies look good?" cried Flossie.

"And I guess they'll eat just as good as they look," was Freddie's comment.

Just then Nan's foot slipped on a small stone, and she came very near falling down.

"Oh!" cried Flossie and Freddie together.

"Don't drop your cookies, Nan!" came quickly from Bert.

"Oh, if you dropped 'em they'd get all dirty," said Flossie.

"They wouldn't get very dirty," answered Freddie hopefully. "Anyway, we could brush 'em off. They'd be good enough to eat, wouldn't they?" and he looked at Bert.

"I guess they wouldn't get very dirty," answered Bert. "Anyway, Nan didn't drop them. But you'd better be careful, Nan," he went on.

"Don't be so scared, Bert Bobbsey," answered his sister. "I won't drop them."

In a minute more the Bobbsey twins were at the barn where the sugar and molasses cookies Dinah had given them were put in a safe place.

"There are the ropes!" exclaimed Bert, as he pointed to some dangling from a beam near the haymow.

"They're too high to climb!" Nan said, for some of the ropes were fast to the rafters of the barn.

"Oh, we won't climb 'em!" Bert quickly returned, for he knew his mother would never allow this. "We'll just swing on 'em, low down near this pile of hay, so if we fall we can't hurt ourselves."

"I want to swing on a rope, too!" exclaimed Freddie, as he heard what his older brother and sister were talking of. "I like to be a sailor and swing on a rope."

"Not now, Freddie," answered Bert. "The ropes are too high for you and Flossie. You just play around on the barn floor, and you can watch Nan and me swing. Then we'll play steamboat, maybe."

"I want to be the steam, and go puff-puff!" cried Freddie.

"And I want to be the captain and say 'All aboard!'" was Flossie's wish.

"You can take turns," agreed Bert. "Now don't get in our way, Flossie and Freddie. Nan and I want to see how big a swing we can take by holding to the ropes."

"All right. I'll go and see if I can find any eggs," replied Freddie. "Hens lay eggs in the barn."

"Well, if you find a nest don't step in it and break all the eggs," warned Nan.

She and Bert, as Flossie and Freddie went marching around the big barn, climbed up on the pile of hay, and began swinging on the ropes. To and fro swung the older Bobbsey twins.

"Isn't this better than Blueberry Island?" asked Nan.

"Well no, it isn't any better," said Bert; "but it's just as good. Look, I'm going to let go and drop on the hay."

"Be careful and don't hurt yourself!" begged Nan, as she swung to and fro, her feet raised from the hay beneath her, while Bert, also, swayed slowly to and fro.

"Oh, I'll be careful!" Bert promised. "Anyhow, the hay is nice and soft to fall in. I'll make believe I'm a man in the circus, falling from the top of the tent."

He swung a little farther to and fro, and then suddenly cried:

"Here I go!"

"Oh!" screamed Nan, but, really, nothing happened to harm Bert. He just dropped into the pile of soft hay.

"Come on, Nan! You try it! Lots of fun!" laughed Bert as he scrambled up and made for his rope again.

Nan said "no" at first, but when Bert had

swung once more and again dropped into the hay, she took her turn. Into the hay she plunged, and sank down to her shoulders in the soft, dried grass.

"Come on—let's do it some more!" laughed Bert. Then he and his older sister had lots of fun swinging on the ropes and dropping into a pile of hay.

"I wonder what Flossie and Freddie are doing," said Bert, after they had had about an hour of this fun. "I haven't seen them for a long while."

"Maybe they found a hen's nest and took the eggs to the house," said Nan. "They'd do that."

"Yes, if they found one," agreed Bert. "Well, we'll see where they are after I take another swing. And I'm going to take a big one."

"So will I!" decided Nan. "Oh, it's just as nice as Blueberry Island or on the deep, blue sea, isn't it, Bert?"

"It is when we play this way—yes. But just watch me."

"Here come Flossie and Freddie now!" exclaimed Nan, as she glanced at her older brother, who was taking a firm hold of the rope for his big swing. The two smaller twins, at this moment, came into the barn through the door that led to the cow stable.

"Where have you been?" asked Nan, as she watched Bert get ready for his swing.

"Oh, we had fun," said Flossie.

"And I squirted water, out where the horse drinks," added Freddie.

"I hope you didn't get wet!" exclaimed Nan. "If you did ——"

"Well, I have on a dirty waist, so it won't hurt me any if I am wet," said Freddie calmly. "I want to swing like that, Bert," he added. "Give me a swing!"

"After I've had my turn I'll give you and Flossie each one," promised Nan. "Watch me, Bert!" she called.

Off the mow swung Nan, clinging to the swaying rope with both hands.

"Come on—let's both let go together and see who falls into the hay first!" proposed Bert.

"All right!" agreed Nan.

"One, two, three!" cried Bert. "Ready! Let go!"

He and Nan let go of the ropes at the same time. Together they dropped down to the hay—and then something happened! The two older Bobbsey children jumped too near the edge of the mow, where the hay was piled in a big roll, like a great feather bed bolster, over the top rail. And Bert and Nan, in their drop, caused a big pile of hay—almost a wagonload—to slip from the mow and down to the barn floor. And directly underneath were Flossie and Freddie!

Down on the two little twins fell Bert and Nan and the big pile of dried grass, and, in an instant, the two golden heads were buried out of sight on the barn floor in a large heap of hay.

CHAPTER II

DIGGING OUT

"Oh, Bert Bobbsey! look what you did," cried Nan.

She picked herself up from the barn floor, to which she had slid after having come down with the pile of hay, with her brother, right where Flossie and Freddie had been playing a moment before.

"Look what you did!" she cried again.

"I didn't do it any more than you did!" exclaimed Bert. "But where is Flossie? And where's Freddie?" He looked around, not seeing the smaller twins, and not having noticed exactly what had happened to them. "Where are they, Nan?"

"Under the hay, and we've got to dig 'em out! I'll get the pitchfork. That's what Sam does when he gets the hay to feed the horse. I can dig out Flossie and Freddie!" cried Nan.

She started to run across the barn floor, but was stopped by a call from Bert.

"Don't do that!" he said.

"What?" she asked.

"Don't get the pitchfork! It's sharp and might hurt Flossie and Freddie. I'll pull the hay off with my hands. You go and tell mother or Dinah! Somebody's got to help! There's 'most a whole load of hay on 'em I guess!"

And indeed it was a large part of the pile of hay in the Bobbsey barn that had slid from the mow when Bert jumped on it. And this hay now covered from sight the "little fire-man" and the "little fat fairy," as Daddy Bobbsey called his two little twins.

"Yes, I'll go for Dinah!" cried Nan. "She knows how to dig under the hay, I guess!"

"And I'll start digging now," added Bert, as he began tossing aside the wisps of dried grass that covered his small brother and sister from sight.

And while the rescue of Freddie and Flossie is being arranged for, I will take this chance to tell my new readers something of the four children, about whom I am going to write in this book.

There are other books ahead of this one, and the first is named after the children. It is called "The Bobbsey Twins," and relates some of the early adventures of Bert, Nan, Flossie and Freddie. Those are the names of the twins, as you have already learned.

The Bobbsey family lived in an eastern city called Lakeport, at the head of Lake Metoka. Mr. Bobbsey was in the lumber business and had an office near his lumberyard, which was "down town" as the children called it.

Now I'll tell you just a little about the four children, their friends and something about the other books, and then I'll get on with the story, which I hope you will wish to read.

There were two sets of twins, you see. Bert and Nan were the older. They each had dark brown hair, brown eyes and were rather tall for their age, and not so very fat; though, of late, with all the good times they had had in the country at Blueberry Island and on the deep, blue sea, the older twins were getting stouter. "Fatter," Freddie called it.

Flossie and Freddie were just the opposite of Bert and Nan. The smaller pair of twins were short and stout, and each had light hair, and blue eyes that looked at you, sometimes, in the funniest way you can imagine.

Besides Mr. and Mrs. Bobbsey there was Dinah, the fat, good-natured colored cook, who knew how to make more kinds of cake than you could eat in one day. And then there was Sam Johnson, her husband. Sam worked about the Bobbsey house and barn, looked after the horse and sometimes drove the automobile, though he said he liked a horse better. But the Bobbsey family liked the automobile, so the horse was used down in the lumberyard more often than to take Bert, Nan, Flossie and Freddie for a ride.

The Bobbsey twins had many friends and relations, but I will not take up your time, now, telling you about them. I must not forget, however, to mention Snoop and Snap. Snoop was a fine, big cat, and he was named "Snoop" because he always seemed to be "snooping" into everything, as Dinah said. Snoop didn't do that to be bad, he just wanted

to find out about things. Once he wanted to
find out what was inside an empty tin can,
and so he stuck his head in and he couldn't
get it out until Bert helped him.

Snap was the Bobbsey dog, and he wasn't
called "Snap" because he would snap at you.
No indeed! It was because, when Bert put
a cracker on his dog's nose, the animal would
"snap" it off with a jerk of his head and eat
it—eat the cracker I mean. That was one
reason he was called "Snap." But there were
other reasons, too.

And so the Bobbsey twins lived in a fine
house in a pleasant city and they had lots of
fun. Those of you who have read the other
books know that. They went to the country
and to the seashore, to visit Uncle William
at the latter place, and Uncle Daniel Bobbsey
in the former.

Of course the Bobbsey twins went to school,
and there is a book telling about them there,
and the fun and adventures they had. Later
on they went to "Snow Lodge," and after an
exciting winter, they spent part of the summer on a houseboat.

When Bert, Nan, Flossie and Freddie went to Meadow Brook, which was the country home of Uncle Daniel, the twins never expected very much to happen. But it did, and they talked about it for a long time. Then they came home to have more good times, and, later on, went to a great city. I haven't space, here, to tell you all that happened. You must get the book and read it for yourself.

After that they spent a summer on Blueberry Island, and there were gypsies on the island. Some strange things happened, but the Bobbsey twins enjoyed every hour of their stay, and did not want to come home.

But they had to, of course, and still more strange adventures awaited them. Those you may read about in the book just before this. It is called: "The Bobbsey Twins on the Deep, Blue Sea," and in it is related how the family went on a voyage to an island off the coast of Florida, to rescue a poor, sick boy who had been left there by mistake.

Now they were home once more.

It was almost time for school to open for the fall term, and the twins were playing in

the barn, making the most of the last days
of their vacation, when the accident happened
about the hay, as I have told you.

"Flossie! Freddie! Are you under there?"
called Bert, anxiously, as he threw aside armful after armful of the dried grass. "Are
you down there under the hay?"

He paused a moment to listen for an answer, but none came. If Flossie and Freddie
were there, either they did not hear him or
they were so smothered by the hay that they
could not answer.

"Oh, I hope nothing has happened to them!"
exclaimed Bert, and he began digging away
faster than before.

Certainly it was a large pile of hay to have
fallen on two little children. But then the
hay was soft, and Bert, himself, had often
been buried under a pile in the field. It had
not hurt, but the dust had made him sneeze.

Faster and faster Bert dug away at the hay.
He heard feet pattering on the barn floor back
of him, and, turning, saw Snap, the big dog,
come running in.

"Oh, Snap!" cried Bert, "Flossie and

Freddie are under the hay! Help me dig 'em out!"

"Bow wow!" barked Snap, just as if he understood. Of course he didn't really know what had happened, but he saw Bert digging away and Snap himself knew enough to do that. Often enough he had dug up, with his front paws, a bone he had buried in the hard ground. This digging in the soft hay was easier than that.

So Snap began to paw aside the hay, just as Bert was doing, and while boy and dog were doing this into the barn came fat Dinah, with Nan running ahead of her.

"Whut's dish yeah has happened, Bert? Whut's all dish yeah I heah Nan say?" demanded the black cook. "Whut you done gone an' done to yo' l'il broth' an' sistah? De pooh l'il honey lambs!"

"I didn't do anything!" declared Bert. "I was swinging on a rope, over the haymow, and so was Nan. And Flossie and Freddie were playing on the barn floor under the mow. I fell on the hay and so did Nan, and a whole lot of it slid down and fell on top of Flossie and Freddie and—and—now they're down under there, I guess!"

"Good land ob massy!" exclaimed Dinah. "Dat suah is a lot to happen to mah poor l'il lambkins! Where is you, Flossie? Where is you, Freddie?" she cried.

There was no answer.

"Oh, Dinah! do get them out," begged Nan.

"I will, honey! I will!" exclaimed the colored woman.

"Shall I go to get Sam?" Nan wanted to know. "Mother isn't at home," she added to Bert. "She went over to Mrs. Black's. Oh, maybe we can't ever get Flossie and Freddie out!"

"Hush yo' talk laik dat!" cried Dinah. "Co'se we git 'em out! We kin do it. No need to git Sam. Come on now, Bert an' Nan! Dig as fast as yo' kin make yo' hands fly!"

Dinah bent over and began tossing aside the hay as Bert had been doing. Nan also helped, and Snap—well he meant to help, but he got in the way more than he did anything else, and Bert tried to send his dog out, but Snap would not go.

Faster and faster worked Dinah, Nan and Bert, and soon the big pile of hay, which had fallen on Flossie and Freddie grew smaller. It was being stacked on another part of the floor.

"Maybe I'd better go and telephone to daddy!" suggested Nan, when the hay pile had been made much smaller. "You don't see anything of them yet, do you Dinah?" she asked anxiously.

"No, not yet, honey! But I soon will. We's 'most to de bottom ob de heap. No use worritin' yo' pa. We'll git Freddie and Flossie out all right!"

Bert was tossing aside the hay so fast that his arms seemed like the spokes of a wheel going around. He felt that it was partly his fault that the hay had fallen on his little brother and sister.

"Now we'll git 'em!" cried Dinah, after a bit. "I see de barn flo' in one place. Come on out, chilluns!" she cried. "Come on out, Flossie an' Freddie! We's dug de hay offen yo' now! Come on out!"

Indeed the hay pile was now so small at

the place where it had slid from the mow, that it would not have hidden Snap, to say nothing of covering the two Bobbsey twins.

But something seemed to be wrong. There were no little fat legs or chubby arms sticking out. The little Bobbsey twins were not in sight, though nearly all the hay had been moved aside.

Bert, Nan and Dinah gazed at the few wisps remaining. Then, in a queer voice Nan said:

"Why—why! They're not there!"

CHAPTER III

THE WASHINGTON CHILDREN

There was no doubt of it. Flossie and Freddie were not under the pile of hay that had fallen on them. The hay had all been cast aside now, so far away from the place where it had fallen that it could not serve for a hiding place. And Bert and Nan could see the bare floor of the barn.

"Where are they?" asked Bert, looking in surprise at Nan. "Where are Flossie and Freddie?"

"Dat's whut I wants to know!" declared Dinah. "Where is dey? Has yo' all been playin' a trick on ole Dinah?" and she looked sadly at Bert and Nan.

"Playing a trick?" cried Nan.

"We didn't play any trick!" exclaimed Bert. "Flossie and Freddie were down under that hay!"

"But they're not there now!" went on Nan.

"No," said Dinah, as she poked aside some of the wisps of hay with her foot. "Dey isn't heah now, an' where is dey? Dat's whut I'se askin' yo' all, Bert an' Nan? Where is dem two little lambkins?"

Bert looked at Nan and Nan looked at Bert. It was a puzzle. What had become of Flossie and Freddie between the time they disappeared under the sliding pile of hay and now, when it had been cleared away to another part of the barn.

"I saw them playing on the floor," said Nan. "Then, when Bert and I let go the ropes and jumped in the mow, a lot of hay came down all at once, and then I—I didn't see Flossie and Freddie any more. They surely were under the hay!"

"Yes," agreed Bert, "they were. But they aren't here now. Maybe they fell down through the floor!" he added hopefully. "The cow stable is under this part of the barn."

"Yes, but there isn't any hole in the barn floor here," said Nan. "And the cracks aren't big enough for Flossie and Freddie to slip through."

"No, dey didn't go t'rough de flo', dat's suah!" exclaimed Dinah. "It's mighty queer! I guess yo' all had best go call Sam," she went on to Nan. Mebby he know something 'bout dish yeah barn dat I don't know. Go git Sam an'——"

Just then there came a joyous shout from the big barn doors behind Nan, Bert and Dinah.

"Here we are! Here we are! Oh, we fooled you! We fooled you!" cried two childish voices, and there stood the missing Flossie and Freddie, hay in their fluffy, golden hair, hay hanging down over their blue eyes, and hay stuck over their clothes.

"Here we are!" cried Freddie. "Did you was lookin' for us?"

"I should say we did was!" cried Bert, laughing, now, at Freddie's queer way of speaking, for, though the little fireman usually spoke quite properly, he sometimes went wrong.

"Where have you been?" asked Nan. "And how did you get out?"

"We crawled out from under the hay when it fell on us," explained Flossie. "Then Freddie says let's play hide and coop and we climbed up the little ladder and went up in the haymow and then we slid out of the little window and got outside the barn and then we just hid an' waited to see what you'd do." By this time Flossie was out of breath, having said all this without pause.

"But you didn't come after us," said Freddie, "and so we came to see where you were. And we fooled you, didn't we? We fooled you bad."

"I should say you did!" cried Bert. "We were digging the hay away. I thought you'd be away down underneath."

"We were," went on Flossie. "But we wiggled out, an' you didn't see us wiggle."

"No," agreed Nan, "we didn't see you. But, oh, I'm so glad you are all right!" she cried, and she hugged Flossie in her arms. "You aren't hurt, are you?"

"No. but I was tickled." said Flossie. "The

hay did tickle me in my nose, and I wanted to sneeze."

"But I wouldn't let her!" explained Freddie. "I held my hand over her nose so she couldn't sneeze."

"I tried hard so I wouldn't," said Flossie, "and Freddie helped me. It feels awful funny not to sneeze when you want to. It tickles!"

"And the hay tickled me," went on Freddie. "It's ticklin' me now. There's some down my back," and he wiggled and twisted as he stood in the middle of the barn floor. Snap, the big dog, put his head to one side, and cocked up his ears, looking at the two smaller twins as if asking what it was all about, and what the digging in the hay was all for.

"Well, it's mighty lucky laik dat it wasn't no wuss!" exclaimed fat Dinah, with a sigh of relief. "I suah was clean skairt out ob mah seben senses when yo' come runnin' into mah kitchen, Nan, an' says as how Flossie an' Freddie was buried under de hay!"

"And they were!" said Nan. "I saw the hay go down all over them."

"So did I!" added Bert.

"But we wiggled out and hid so we could
fool you!" laughed Freddie. "Didn't you see
us crawl out?"

"No," answered Bert, "I didn't. If I had
I wouldn't have dug so hard."

"Ouch! Something tickles me awful!" complained Freddie, twisting around as though he
wanted to work his way out of his clothes.
"Maybe there's a hay-bug down my back!" he
went on.

"Good land of massy!" cried Dinah, catching him up in her arms. "Yo' come right
in de house wif me, honey lamb, an' ole
Dinah'll undress yo' an' git at de bug—if dey
is one!"

"I guess we've had enough fun in the barn,"
said Nan. "I don't want to play here any
more."

"I guess we'll have to put back the hay we
knocked down," said Bert. That was one of
the Bobbsey rules—to put things back the way
they had been at first, after their play was
done.

"Yes, we must put the hay up in the mow
again," agreed Nan. "Daddy wouldn't like

to have us leave it on the floor. I'll help you, Bert, 'cause I helped knock it down."

Dinah led the two younger twins off to the kitchen, with a promise of a molasses cookie each and a further promise to Freddie that she would take out of his clothes whatever it was tickling his back—a hay-bug or some of the dried wisps of grass.

Bert and Nan had not long been working at stacking the hay back in place before Sam came in. He had heard what had happened from Dinah, his wife, and he said, most kindly:

"Run along an' play, Bert an' Nan! I'll put back de hay fo' yo' all. 'Tain't much, an' it won't take me long."

"Thank you, Sam!" said Bert. "It's more fun playing outdoors to-day than stacking hay in a barn."

"Are you very sure you don't mind doing it, Sam?" asked Nan, for she wanted to "play fair."

"Oh, I don't mind!" exclaimed the good-natured Sam. "Hop along!"

"Didn't you ever like to play outdoors,

Sam?" questioned Bert, as he and Nan started to leave the barn.

"Suah I did," answered Sam. "When I was a youngster like you I loved to go fishin' and swimmin' in the ole hole down by the crick."

"Oh, Sam, did you like to swim?" went on the Bobbsey boy quickly.

"I suah did, Bert. Down in our pa'ts I was considered the bestes' swimmer there."

"Some day I'm going to see you, Sam," declared Bert. "Maybe you could teach me some new strokes."

"I doan know about that, Bert. You see, I ain't quite so limber as what I used to be when I was your age or jest a little older. Now you jest hop along, both of you, and enjoy yourselves."

So Nan and Bert went out to find some other way of having fun. They wanted to have all the good times they could, as school would soon begin again.

"But we'll have a vacation at Thanksgiving and Christmas and New Year's," said Nan, as she and her brother talked it over.

"Thanksgiving's a long way off," said Bert, with a sigh.

The two children were walking along the side path toward the front yard when suddenly Snap, their dog, gave a savage growl. It was the kind of growl he never gave unless he happened to be angry, and Bert knew, right away, something must be wrong.

"What is it, Snap? A tramp?" asked the boy, looking around. Often Snap would growl this way at tramps who might happen to come into the yard. Now there may be good tramps, as well as bad ones, but Snap never stopped to find out which was which. He just growled, and if that didn't scare away the tramp then Snap ran at him. And no tramp ever stood after that. He just ran away.

But now neither Bert nor Nan could see any tramp, either in the yard or in the street in front of the house. Snap, though, kept on growling deep down in his throat, and then, suddenly, the children saw what the matter was. A big dog was digging a hole under the fence to get into the Bobbsey yard. The gate was closed, and though the dog might have jumped the fence, he didn't. He was digging a hole underneath. And Snap saw him. That's why Snap growled.

"Oh, Bert! Look!" cried Nan.

As she spoke the dog managed to get through the hole he had dug, and into the Bobbsey yard he popped. But he did not stay there long. Before he could run toward Bert and Nan, if, indeed, he had that notion, Snap had leaped toward the unwelcome visitor.

Snap growled and barked in such a brave, bold way that the other dog gave one long howl, and then back through the hole he wiggled his way, faster than he had come in. But fast as he wiggled out, he was not quick enough, for Snap nipped the end of the big dog's tail and there was another howl.

"Good boy!" cried Bert to his dog, as Snap came back to him, wagging his tail, having first made sure, however, that the strange dog was running down the street. "Good, old Snap!"

And Snap wagged his tail harder than ever,

for he liked to be told he had been good and had done something worth while.

"I wonder what that dog wanted?" asked Nan.

"I don't know," answered Bert. "He was a strange one. But he didn't stay long!"

"Not with our Snap around!" laughed Nan.

The two older Bobbsey twins were wondering what they could do next to have a good time, when they heard their mother's voice calling to them from the side porch. She had come back from a little visit to a lady down the street, and had heard all about the accident to Flossie and Freddie.

"Ho, Nan! Ho, Bert! I want you!" called Mrs. Bobbsey.

"I guess she's going to scold us for making the hay slide on Flossie and Freddie," said Bert, rather anxiously.

"Well, we couldn't help it," replied his sister. "We didn't know it was so slippery. Yes, Mother; we're coming!" she answered, as Mrs. Bobbsey called again.

But, to the relief of Nan and Bert, their mother did not scold them. She just said:

"You must be a little more careful when you're playing where Flossie and Freddie are. They are younger than you, and don't so well know how to look out for themselves. You must look out for them. But now I want you to go down to daddy's office."

"What do you want us to do?" asked Nan.

"Here is a letter that he ought to have right away," went on Mrs. Bobbsey. "It came to the house by mistake. It should have gone to daddy's lumber office, but the postman left it while I was out, and Dinah was out in the barn with you children, so she could not tell him to carry it on down town. So I wish you'd take it to daddy. He has been expecting it for some time. It's about some business, and I don't want to open the letter and telephone what's in it. But if you two will just run down with it——"

"Of course we will!" cried Bert. "It'll be fun!"

"And may we stay a little while?" asked Nan.

"Yes, if you don't bother daddy. Here is the letter."

A little later Nan and Bert were in their father's office. The clerks knew the children and smiled at them, and the stenographer, who wrote Mr. Bobbsey's letters on the clicking typewriter machine, took the twins through her room into their father's private office.

As the door opened, Bert and Nan saw a strange man talking to Mr. Bobbsey. But what interested them more than this was the sight of two children—a boy and a girl about their own age—in their father's private office. The boy and girl were sitting on chairs, looking at the very same lumber books—those with pictures of big woods in them—that Nan and Bert often looked at themselves.

Mr. Bobbsey glanced up as the door opened. He saw his two older twins, and, smiling at them, said:

"Come in, Nan and Bert. I want you to meet these Washington children!"

CHAPTER IV

MISS POMPRET'S CHINA

BERT and Nan looked at one another in some surprise as they stood in the door of their father's private office. What did he mean by saying that they were to come in and meet the "Washington children?" Who were the "Washington children?"

Nan and Bert were soon to know, for their father spoke again.

"Come on in. These are two of my twins, Mr. Martin," he added to the gentleman who was sitting near his desk. The two "Washington children," looked up from the lumber books they had been reading. No, I am wrong, they had not been reading them—only looking at the pictures.

"Two of your twins?" repeated Mr. Martin, with a smile. "Do you mean to say you have more twins at home?"

"Oh, yes, another set. Smaller than these.

I wish you would see Flossie and Freddie.
Come here, Bert and Nan. This is my friend,
Mr. Martin," he continued, "and these are his
children, Billy and Nell. They live in Washington, D. C."

So that was what Mr. Bobbsey meant. At
first, Nan said afterward, she had a little notion that her father might have meant the boy
and girl were the children of General George
Washington. But a moment's thought told
Nan that this could not be. General Washington's children, supposing him to have had any,
would have been grown up into old men and
women and would have passed away long ago.
But Billy and Nell Martin lived in Washington, District of Columbia (which is what the
letters D. C. stand for) and, Bert and Nan
knew, Washington was the capital, or chief
city, of the United States.

"Mr. Martin came in to see me on business,"
explained Daddy Bobbsey. "He is traveling
for a lumber firm, and on this trip he brought
his boy and girl with him."

"They aren't twins, though," said Mr. Martin with a nod at Nan and Bert.

"I think it's lovely to be a twin!" said Nell, with a smile at Nan. "Don't you have lots of fun?"

"Yes, we do," Nan said.

"I should think you could have fun in this lumberyard," remarked Billy Martin. "I'd like to live near it."

"Yes, we play in it," said Bert; and now that the "ice had been broken," as the grown folks say, the four children began to feel better acquainted.

"Did you come down for anything special?" asked Mr. Bobbsey of Bert.

"Yes, Daddy. Here's a letter mother gave us for you," the boy answered.

"Oh, this is the one I have been expecting," said Mr. Bobbsey to Mr. Martin. "Now we can talk business. Bert and Nan, don't you want to take Billy and Nell out in the yard and show them the lake? But don't fall in, and don't climb on the lumber," he added.

"Oh, I'd love to look at the lake!" cried Nell.

"And I like to see big piles of lumber," said her brother Billy.

"The children will be all right," said Mr. Bobbsey, in answer to a look from Mr. Martin. "My older twins often play about the lumber-yard, and they'll see that Billy and Nell come to no harm."

So while the two men talked over lumber matters, Bert and Nan showed Billy and Nell the sights of their father's lumberyard, and took the Washington children down to Lake Metoka, where the blue waters sparkled in the sun.

"Oh, this is lovely!" exclaimed Nell. "It's nicer than Washington!"

"Don't you have a lake there?" asked Bert.

"No; but we have the Potomac River," answered Billy. "That's nice, but not as nice as this lake. Now let's go and look at the big piles of lumber."

"Yes, let's," echoed Nell.

The children tossed some chips into the lake, pretending they were boats, and then they walked around the yard to where long boards and planks were stacked into great piles, wait-ing to be taken away on boats or wagons.

Bert asked one of the workmen if they could

play with some of the boards, and, receiving permission to do so, they had fun making something they called a house, and then on a see-saw.

"Oh, I always did love to see-saw!" said the little girl from Washington. "We don't get much of a chance to play that way where I come from."

"We have see-saw rides lots of times down here," answered Nan.

"Well, that's because your father owns a lumberyard, and you can get plenty of boards to use for a see-saw," said Henry.

For an hour or more Bert and Nan entertained the Washington children in the lumberyard, and then, as it was getting close to dinner time, Nan told Bert they had better go back to their father's office.

They found Mr. Martin about to leave. And then Mr. Bobbsey thought of something.

"Look here, Henry!" he exclaimed to his friend, "there's no need of your going back to that hotel. Come out to the house—you and the children—and have dinner with me. I want you and your boy and girl to meet Flossie and Freddie, and I want you to meet Mrs. Bobbsey."

"Well, I'd like to," said Mr. Martin slowly, while the eyes of Nell and Billy glowed in delight. "But, perhaps it might bother your wife."

"Oh, no!" laughed Mr. Bobbsey. "She likes company. I'll telephone out that we're coming, and Dinah, that's our cook, will be delighted to get up something extra. They'll be glad to see you. Come out to the house, all of you, and make me a nice visit. Can't you stay a day or so?"

Eagerly Nan and Bert waited for the answer, for they liked the Washington children very much.

"Oh, no, we can't stay later than this evening," said Mr. Martin. "I've got other business to look after. But I'll come out to dinner with you."

"Oh, we'll have lots of fun!" whispered Nan to Nell. "You'll just love Flossie—she's so cute!"

"I'll show you my dog Snap," said Bert to Billy. "You ought to have seen him scare a strange dog just before we came down here."

"I like dogs," said Billy. "We could have one in Washington if we had a barn to keep him in."

"We've got a barn," went on Bert. "You ought to have seen what happened there this morning to Flossie and Freddie," and then he told about the little twins having been hidden under the hay.

Mr. Bobbsey's automobile was in the lumberyard, and in this the trip was quickly made to the home of the four twins, after Mrs. Bobbsey had been told, by telephone, that company was coming

Nell and Billy were glad to see Flossie and Freddie, and the six children had fun playing around the house and barn with Snoop and Snap.

Mr. and Mrs. Bobbsey wanted Mr. Martin to stay two or three days with his children, but the Washington lumberman said it could not be done this time.

"I'm on a business trip," he said, "and I can't spend as much time in visiting and pleasure as I'd like, though I am trying to give

Billy and Nell a good time. This is the first time I have ever taken them on a trip with me."

"And we've had such a lovely time!" exclaimed Nell.

"Packs of fun!" added her brother.

"I'm sorry we can't stay longer," went on Mr. Martin. "You folk must come to Washington some day."

"Yes, I expect to," said Mr. Bobbsey. "I've been counting on going there some day on some business matters."

"Well, when you come be sure to bring the children," said the father of Nell and Billy. "I think they would enjoy seeing the White House, the big Capitol building, the Congressional Library, Washington's home at Mt. Vernon and places like that."

"Could we see the Washington Monument?" asked Nan. She remembered looking at a picture of that in her geography.

"Oh, yes, I'd show you that, too," said Mr. Martin.

"And could we see the Potomac River?" Bert wanted to know.

"Surely!" laughed Billy's father. "I'll show you all the sights of Washington if you'll come and pay me a visit—all you Bobbsey twins!" he added.

"I wish we could go!" sighed Nan.

"Perhaps you can," said her father.

"Have you got any hay in Wash'ton?" asked Freddie, suddenly, and every one else laughed except himself and Flossie.

"Oh, I guess I could find enough hay for you and your little sister to hide under," answered Mr. Martin with a laugh, for he had heard the story of what had happened in the barn.

A little later Mr. Martin and his boy and girl had to leave. They said "good-bye," and while the father of the Washington children again asked Mr. and Mrs. Bobbsey to come to visit him at his home, Nell and Billy whispered to Nan and Bert:

"Be sure and come, and bring Flossie and Freddie with you!"

"We will!" promised Nan, but neither she nor Bert guessed what a queer little adventure they were soon to have in Washington.

A few days later school opened, and the Bobbsey twins had to go back to their class-rooms. At first they did not like it, after the long, joyous vacation on the deep, blue sea, but their teachers were kind, and finally the twins began to feel that, after all, school was not such a bad place.

Thanksgiving Day came, bringing a little vacation period, and after church in the morn-ing, the Bobbsey twins went home to eat roast turkey and cranberry sauce. Then they went out to play with some of their boy and girl friends, having lots of fun in the barn and yard.

"But don't slide any more hay down on Flossie and Freddie!" begged Mrs. Bobbsey.

"We won't!" promised Bert and Nan, and they kept their word.

It was about a week after Thanksgiv-ing, and Bert and Nan were on their way home from school one day, when, as they passed a red brick house on the street next to theirs, they saw, standing on the porch, a pleasant-faced, elderly lady who was looking up and down the avenue.

"That's Miss Pompret," said Nan to Bert "I heard mother say she was very rich."

"Is she?" asked Bert. "She looks kind of funny."

"That's 'cause she isn't married," returned Nan. "Some folks call her an old maid, but I don't think she's very old, even if her hair is white. Her face looks nice."

"Yes, but she looks kind of worried now," said Bert. "That's the way mother looks when she's worried."

They were in front of the house now, and could see Miss Pompret quite plainly. Certainly the elderly lady did look as though something troubled her.

"Good afternoon, Miss Pompret!" called Nan, as she was about to pass by. Bert took off his cap and bowed.

"Oh, you're half of the Bobbsey twins, aren't you?" asked Miss Pompret, with a smile. "I often see you go past. I only wish you were a little bigger."

"Bigger? Why?" asked Bert, in some surprise.

"Why, then," explained Miss Pompret,

"you might take this letter to the post-office for me. It's very important, and I want it to go out on this mail, but I can't go to the post-office myself. If you Bobbsey twins were bigger I should ask you to take it. Tell me, is the other set of twins larger than you two?"

"No'm; they're smaller," explained Nan. "Flossie and Freddie are lots littler than we are."

"But we're big enough to take the letter to the post-office for you, Miss Pompret," said Bert. He had often heard his father and mother speak of this neighbor, and the kindnesses she had done.

"Are you sure you are big enough to go to the post-office for me?" asked Miss Pompret.

"We often go for daddy and mother," said Nan.

"Well, then, if you think your mother wouldn't mind, I would like, very much, to have you go," said Miss Pompret. "The letter is very important, but I can not take it myself, as I have company, and I have no one, just now, who can leave. I thought I might see some large boy on the street, but——"

"I'm big enough!" exclaimed Bert.

"Yes, I believe you are!" agreed the elderly lady, looking at him through her glasses. "Well, I shall be very thankful to you and your sister if you will mail the letter for me. And, on your way back, stop and let me know that you dropped it in the post-office all right."

"We will!" promised Bert, and Nan nodded her head in agreement with him. Miss Pompret handed over the letter, which was in a large envelope. Nan and Bert were soon at the post-office with it.

The white-haired lady was waiting for them on the porch as they came back along the street.

"Won't you come in, just for a minute?" she asked, smiling kindly at them. "My maid has just baked a chocolate cake, and I don't believe your mother would mind if you each had a piece."

"Oh, no'm—she wouldn't mind at all!" said Bert quickly.

"We like chocolate cake," said Nan, "but we didn't go to the post-office for that!"

"Bless your heart, child, I know you didn't!" laughed their new friend. "Please come in!"

The chocolate cake was all Bert and Nan hoped it would be, and besides that Miss Pompret set out on the table for them each a glass of milk. They looked around the beautiful but old-fashioned room, noting the dark mahogany furniture, the cut glass on the sideboard, and, over in one corner, a glass cupboard, through the clear doors of which could be seen some china dishes.

Miss Pompret saw Nan looking at this set of china, and the elderly lady smiled as she said:

"Isn't it beautiful?"

"Yes," said Nan, softly. "I love pretty dishes."

"And these are my greatest treasure," said Miss Pompret. "I am very proud of them. They have been in my family over a hundred years. But there is a sad story about it—a very sad story about the old Pompret china." And the lady's face clouded.

"Did somebody break it?" asked Bert. Once

he had broken a plate of which his mother was very proud, and he remembered how sad she felt.

"No, my china wasn't broken," said Miss Pompret. "In fact, there is a sort of mystery about it."

"Oh, please tell me!" begged Nan. "I like nice dishes and I like stories."

She and Bert looked at the closet of choice china dishes. Children though they were, they could see that the plates, cups, saucers and other dishes were not like the kind set on their table every day.

What could Miss Pompret mean about a "mystery" connected with her set of china?

CHAPTER V

"WHAT A LOT OF MONEY!"

Bert and Nan sat up very straight on the chairs in Miss Pompret's dining room, and looked first at her and then at the china closet with its shiny, glass doors. Miss Pompret sat up very straight, too, in her chair, and she, also, looked first from Nan and Bert to the wonderful china, which seemed made partly of egg shells, so fine it was and pretty.

Miss Pompret's dining room was one in which it seemed every one had to sit up straight, and in which every chair had to be in just the right place, where the table legs must keep very straight, too, and where not even a corner of a rug dared to be turned up. In fact it was a very straight, old-fashioned but very beautiful dining room, and Miss Pompret herself was an old-fashioned but beautiful lady.

54

"Now if you will sit very still, and not move, I'll bring out some pieces of my china set and show them to you," said Miss Pompret. "You were so kind as to take the letter to the post-office for me when I could not go myself, that I feel I ought to reward you in some way."

"The chocolate cake was enough," said Nan.

"Yes, it was awful good!" sighed Bert.

"Mother told you not to say 'awful,'" interposed Bert's sister.

"Oh, well, I mean it was terribly nice!" exclaimed the boy.

"I'm glad you liked it," went on Miss Pompret with a smile. "But I must not keep you too long, or your mother will be wondering what has become of you. But I thought you, Nan, would be interested in seeing beautiful china. You'll have a home of your own, some day, and nothing is nicer in a nice home than beautiful dishes."

"I know that!" cried Nan. "My mamma has some very beautiful dishes, and once in a great while she lets me look them over. Sometimes, too, we have them on the table—when it's some special occasion like a birthday or visitors."

"I don't much like to see the real nice dishes on a table," remarked Bert. "I'm always afraid that I'll break one of them, and then I know my mother would feel pretty bad over it."

"You must be careful, my boy. You can't handle nice china as you can your baseball or your football," said Miss Pompret, with a smile.

"Well, I guess they couldn't treat dishes like baseballs and footballs!" cried Nan. "Just think of throwing a sugar bowl up into the air or hitting it with a bat, or kicking a teapot all around the lots!"

"That certainly wouldn't be very nice," said Miss Pompret.

She went over to the closet, unlocked the glass doors, and set some of the rare pieces out on the lace cover of the dining room table. Bert and Nan saw that Miss Pompret handled each piece as though it might be crushed, even in her delicate hands, which were almost as white and thin as a piece of china.

"This is the wonderful Pompret tableware," went on the old lady. It has been in my family over a hundred years. My great-grandfather had it, and now it has come to me. I have had it a number of years, and I think more of it than anything else I have. Of course, if I had any little children I would care for them more than for these dishes," went on Miss Pompret. "But I'm a lonely old lady, and you neighborhood children are the only ones I have," and she smiled rather wistfully at Nan and Bert.

Carefully dish after dish was taken from the closet and set out for the Bobbsey twins to look at. They did not venture to so much as touch one. The china seemed too easily broken for that.

"I should think you'd have to be very careful when you washed those dishes," remarked Nan, as she saw how light glowed through the side of one of the thin cups.

"Oh, I am," answered Miss Pompret. "No one ever washes this set but me. My maid is very careful, but I would not allow her to touch a single piece. I don't use it very often. Only when some old and dear friends come to see me is the Pompret china used. And then I am sorry to say, I can not use the whole set."

"Why not?" asked Bert. "Are you afraid they'll break it?"

"Oh no," and Miss Pompret smiled. "I'm not afraid of that. But you see I haven't the whole set, so I can't show it all. One of the sorrows of my life is that part of my beautiful set of china is missing."

"There's a lot of it, though," added Bert, as he saw a number of shelves covered with the rare plates, cups and saucers.

"Yes, but the sugar bowl and cream pitcher are missing," went on Miss Pompret, with a shake of her white head. "They were beautiful. But, alas! they are missing." And she sighed deeply.

"Where are they?" asked Nan.

"Ah, that's the mystery I am going to tell you about," said Miss Pompret. "It isn't a very big story, and I won't keep you long. It isn't often I get a chance to tell it, so you must forgive an old lady for keeping you from your play," and again she smiled, in rather a sad fashion, at Nan and Bert.

"Oh, we like it here!" exclaimed Nan quickly.

"It's lots of fun!" added Bert. "I like to hear about a mystery."

"Well," began Miss Pompret, "as I told you, this set of china has been in our family over a hundred years. It was made in England, and each piece has the mark of the man who made it. See, this is what I mean."

She turned over one of the cups and showed the Bobbsey twins where, on the bottom, there was the stamp, in blue, of some animal in a circle of gold.

"That is the mark of the Waredon factory, where this china was made," went on Miss Pompret. "Only china made by Mr. Waredon can have this mark on it."

"It looks like our dog Snap," said Bert.

"Oh, no!" laughed Miss Pompret. "That is supposed to be the British lion. Mr. Waredon took that as a trade-mark, and at the top of the golden circle, with the blue lion inside, you can see the letter 'J' while at the bottom is the letter 'W.' They stand for the name Jonathan Waredon, in whose English factory the china was made. Each piece has this mark on it, nad no other make of china in the world can be rightfully marked like that.

"Well, now about the mystery. Some years ago, before you children were born, I lived in another city. I had the china set there with me, and then it was complete. I had the cream pitcher and the sugar bowl. One day a ragged man came to the house. He was very ragged and poor. I suppose you would call him a tramp.

"The cook I then had felt sorry for him, and let him come into the kitchen to have something to eat. As it happened, part of my rare china set was on a table in the same room. I was getting ready to wash it myself, as I would let no one else touch it.

"Well, when I came out to wash my beautiful dishes the sugar bowl and cream pitcher of the set were gone. They had been on the table when the tramp was eating the lunch the cook gave him, but now they could not be found. The cook and I looked all over for them—we searched the house, in fact, but never found them."

"Who took them?" asked Bert, eagerly.

"Well, my dear boy, I have never found out. The cook always said the tramp put the sugar bowl and cream pitcher in his pocket when her back was turned to get him a cup of coffee. At any rate, when he was gone the two pieces were gone also, and while I do not want to think badly of any one, I have come to believe that the tramp took my rare dishes."

"Didn't you ever see him again?" asked Nan.

"No, my dear, never, as far as I know."

"And did you never find the dishes?" Bert wanted to know.

"Never. I advertised for them. I inquired if any boys in the neighborhood might have slipped in and taken them for a joke, but I never found them. To this day," went on Miss Pompret, "I have never again set eyes on my cream pitcher and sugar bowl. They disappeared as completely and suddenly as though they had fallen down a hole in the earth. The tramp may have taken them; but what would he do with just two pieces? They were too frail for him to use. A man like that would want heavy dishes. Perhaps he knew how valuable they were and perhaps he intended asking a reward for bringing them back. But I never heard from him.

"So that is why my rare set of Pompret china is not complete. The two pieces are missing and I would give a hundred dollars this minute if I could get them back!"

"A—a hundred dollars!" exclaimed Bert.

"Yes, my boy. If some one would get me that sugar bowl and pitcher, with the mark of the lion in a golden circle, and the initials 'J' at the top and 'W' at the bottom, I would willingly pay one hundred dollars," said Miss Pompret.

"A—a whole hundred dollars!" gasped Bert. "What a lot of money!"

CHAPTER VI

WONDERFUL NEWS

Miss Alicia Pompret began putting back in the glass-doored closet the pieces of rare china that had the blue lion in a circle of gold and the initials "J. W." on the bottom of each piece. Nan and Bert watched her, and saw how carefully her white hands took up each plate and cup.

"A hundred dollars!" murmured Bert again. "I'd like to have all that money. I'd buy— er—I'd buy a goat!"

"A goat!" exclaimed Miss Pompret.

"Yes," went on Bert. "Freddie nearly bought one once, when we went to the big city, but mother wouldn't let him keep it. Now we're back home; and if I had a hundred dollars I'd buy a goat."

"Well, if you can find my sugar bowl and pitcher I'll be glad to pay you a hundred dol-

lars," said Miss Pompret with a smile at Bert.
"But I don't know that I'd like a goat," she
added.

"Do you really mean you'd pay a hundred
dollars for two china dishes?" asked Nan, her
eyes big with wonder.

"Yes, my dear," said Miss Pompret. "Of
course if they were just two ordinary dishes,
such as these," and she pointed to some on a
side table, "they would not be worth a hundred
dollars. But I need just those two pieces—
the pitcher and sugar bowl—to make my rare
set of china complete again. So if you children should happen to come across them, bring
them to me and I'll pay you a hundred dollars.
But, of course," she added, "they must be the
pieces that match my set—they must have the
lion mark on the underside. However," she
concluded with a sigh, "I don't suppose you'll
ever find them. The tramp must have broken
them many long years ago. I'll never see them
again."

"Did you know the tramp's name?" asked
Bert.

"Bless you, of course not!" laughed Miss

Pompret. "Tramps hardly ever tell their names, and when they do, they don't give the right one. No, I'm sure I'll never see my beautiful dishes again. Sometimes I dream that I shall, and I am disappointed when I awaken. But now I mustn't keep you children any longer. I've told you my little mystery story, and I hope you liked it."

"Yes, we did, very much," answered Nan. "Only it's too bad!"

"You aren't sure the tramp took the dishes, are you?" asked Bert.

"No; and that is where the mystery comes in," said Miss Pompret. "Perhaps he didn't, and, maybe, in some unexpected way, I'll find them again. I hope I do, or that some one does, and I'll pay the hundred dollars to whoever does."

"My, that's a lot of money!" murmured Bert again, when he and Nan were once more on their way home, having said good-bye to Miss Pompret. "I wish we could find those dishes."

"So do I," agreed Nan. "But don't call 'em dishes, Bert."

"What are they?" her brother wanted to know.

"Why, they're rare china. When I grow up I'm going to have a set just like Miss Pompret's."

"With the dog on the bottom?"

" 'Tisn't a *dog,* it's a *lion!*" exclaimed Nan.

"Well, it looks like our dog Snap," declared Bert.

They ran on home to find their mother out at the gate looking up and down the street for them.

"Are you children just getting home from school?" asked Mrs. Bobbsey. "Were you kept in for doing something wrong?"

"Oh, no'm!" exclaimed Nan. "We went to see Miss Pompret."

"And she's going to give us a hundred dollars if we find two of her dishes!" exclaimed Bert.

"My! What's all this?" asked his mother, laughing.

" 'Tisn't dishes! It's rare china," said Nan, and then, between them, she and Bert told the story of the little favor they had done for

Miss Pompret, and how she had invited them in, given them cake and milk, and told them the mystery story.

"Well, you had quite a visit," said Mrs. Bobbsey. "Miss Pompret is a dear lady, rather queer, perhaps, but very kind and a good neighbor. I am glad you did her a favor. I have heard, before, about her china, and knew she had some other rare and old-fashioned things in her house. I have been there once or twice. Now I want you to go to the store for me. Sam is away and Dinah needs some things for supper."

"I want to go to the store, too!" exclaimed Freddie, who came around the corner of the house just then, with his face and hands covered with mud.

"Oh, my dear child! what have you been doing?" cried his mother.

"Oh, just makin' pies," answered Freddie, rubbing one cheek with a grimy hand. "I made the pies and Flossie put 'em in the oven to bake. We made an oven out of some bricks. But we didn't really eat the pies," he added, " 'cause they were only mud."

"You look as though you had tried to eat them," laughed Nan. "Come, Freddie, I'll wash you clean."

"No, I want to go to the store!" he cried.

"So do I!" chimed in the voice of Flossie, as she, too, marched around the corner of the house, dirtier, if possible, than her little twin brother. "If Freddie goes to the store, I want to go with him!" Flossie cried.

"All right," answered Bert. "You go and wash Flossie and Freddie, Nan, and I'll get the express wagon and we'll pull them to the store with us. Then we can put the groceries in the wagon and bring them back that way."

"That will be nice," put in Mrs. Bobbsey. "I'll go and see just what Dinah wants. Run along with Nan, Flossie and Freddie, and let her wash you nice and clean."

This just suited the smaller twins, and soon they were being made, by Nan's use of soap and water in the bath room, to look a little less like mud pies. While Bert got out the express wagon, Snap, the big dog, saw his little master, and jumped about, barking in joy.

"I don't care if that is a lion on the back

of Miss Pompret's dishes," murmured Bert, as he put a piece of carpet in the wagon for Flossie and Freddie to sit on, "it looks just like you, Snap. And I wonder if I could ever find that milk pitcher and sugar bowl and get that hundred dollars. I don't guess I could, but I'd like to awful much. No, I mustn't say 'awful,' but I'd like to a terrible lot. A hundred dollars is a pack of money!"

Down the street Nan and Bert pulled Flossie and Freddie in the little express wagon, with Snap running on ahead and barking in delight. This was the best part of the day for him—when the children came home from school. Flossie and Freddie came first, and then Nan and Bert, and then the fun started.

"Now don't run too fast!" exclaimed Flossie, as the express wagon began to bounce over the uneven sidewalk.

"Oh, yes, let's go real fast!" cried Freddie. "Let's go as fast as the fire engines go."

"We can't run as fast as that, Freddie," declared Nan, who was almost out of breath. "We'll just run regular."

And then she and Bert pulled the younger twins around for a little ride in the express wagon before they did the errand on which they had been sent.

"I had a letter from Mr. Martin to-day," said Mr. Bobbsey at the supper table that evening. "He asked to be remembered to you," he said to Mrs. Bobbsey. "And Billy and Nell sent their love to you children."

"They got safely back to Washington, did they?" asked Mrs. Bobbsey.

"Yes," her husband answered. "And they said they had had a very nice visit here. They are anxious to have us come to Washington to see them."

"Can we go?" asked Nan.

"Well, perhaps, some day," said her father.

"I'd like to go now," murmured Bert. "Maybe we might see that tramp in Washington, and get back Miss Pompret's dishes."

"Rare china," muttered Nan, half under her breath.

"What tramp is that, and what about Miss Pompret's dishes?" asked Daddy Bobbsey, as he took his cup of tea from Dinah.

Then he had to hear the story of that after-noon's visit of Nan and Bert.

"Oh, I guess Miss Pompret will never see her two china pieces again," said Mr. Bobbsey. "If the tramp took them he must have sold them, if he didn't smash them. So don't think of that hundred dollars, Bert and Nan."

"But couldn't we go to Washington, any-how?" Bert wanted to know.

"Well, not right away, I'm afraid," his father answered. "You have to go to school, you know."

But a few days after that something hap-pened. About eleven o'clock in the morning Bert, Nan, Flossie and Freddie came trooping home. Into the house they burst with shouts of laughter.

"What's the matter? What is it? Has any-thing happened?" cried Mrs. Bobbsey. "Why are you home from school at such a time of day?"

"There isn't any school," explained Nan.

"No school?" questioned her mother.

"And there won't be any for a month, I guess!" added Bert. "Hurray!"

"What do you mean?" asked his surprised mother. "No school for a month?"

"No, Mother," added Nan. "The steam boiler is broken and they can't heat our room. It got so cold the teacher sent us home."

"An' we came home, too!" added Flossie. "We couldn't stay in our school 'cause our fingers were so cold!"

"Was any one hurt when the boiler burst?" asked Mrs. Bobbsey.

"No," Bert said. "It didn't exactly burst very hard, I guess."

But Mrs. Bobbsey wanted to know just what the trouble was, so she called up the principal of the school on the telephone, and from him learned that the heating boiler of the school had broken, not exactly burst, and that it could no longer heat the rooms.

"It will probably be a month before we can get a new boiler, and until then there will be no more school," he said. "The children will have another vacation."

"A vacation so near Christmas," murmured Mrs. Bobbsey. "I wonder what I can do with my twins?"

Just then the telephone rang, and Mrs. Bobbsey listened. It was Mr. Bobbsey telephoning. He had heard of some accident at the school, and he called up his house, from the lumberyard, to make sure his little fat fairy and fireman, as well as Nan and Bert, were all right.

"Yes, they're home safe," said Mrs. Bobbsey. "But there will be no school for a month."

"Good!" exclaimed Daddy Bobbsey. "That will just suit me and the children, too. I'll be home in a little while, and I have some wonderful news for them!"

"Oh, I wonder what it can be!" exclaimed Nan, when her mother told her what Daddy Bobbsey had said.

CHAPTER VII

ON A TRIP

THE Bobbsey twins could hardly wait for their daddy to come come home after their mother had told them what he said over the telephone.

"Tell me again, Mother, just what he told you!" begged Nan.

"Well, he said he was just as glad as you children were, that there was to be no more school for a month," answered Mrs. Bobbsey. "Though, of course, he was sorry that the steam boiler had broken. And then he said he had some wonderful news to tell us all."

"Oh, I know what it is!" cried Bert.

"What?" asked Nan.

"He's found the tramp that took Miss Pompret's dishes," went on Bert, "and he's got them back—daddy has—and he's going to get the hundred dollars! That's it!"

"Oh, I hardly think so," said Mrs. Bobbsey,

74

with a smile. "I don't believe daddy has caught any tramp."

"They do sometimes sleep in the lumber-yard," remarked Bert.

"Yes, I know," agreed his mother. "But, even if daddy had caught a tramp, it would hardly be the same man who took Miss Pompret's rare pieces of china—the pitcher and sugar bowl. And if it had been anything like that, daddy would have told me over the telephone."

"But what could the wonderful news be?" asked Nan.

"Something too long to talk about until he gets home, I think," answered Mother Bobbsey. "Have patience, daddy will soon be here!"

But of course the Bobbsey twins could not be patient any more than you could if you expected something unusual. They looked at the clock, they ran to the door several times to look down the street to see if their father was coming, and, at last, when Nan had said for about the tenth time: "I wonder what it is!" a step sounded on the front porch.

"There's daddy now!" cried Bert.

Eight feet rushed to the front door, and Mr. Bobbsey was almost overwhelmed by the four twins leaping at him at once.

"What is it?" cried Bert.

"Tell us the wonderful news!" begged Nan.

"Have you got another dog for us?" Flossie wanted to know.

"Did you bring me a new toy fire engine?" cried Freddie.

"Maybe it's a goat!" exclaimed Flossie.

"Now wait a minute! Wait a minute!" laughed Mr. Bobbsey, as he kissed each one in turn. "Sit down and I'll tell you all about it."

He led them into the library, and sat down on a couch, taking Flossie and Freddie up on his knees, while Bert and Nan sat close on either side.

"Now first let me hear all about what happened at school to-day," said Mr. Bobbsey, who had come home to dinner.

"Oh, no!" laughed Nan. "We want to hear the wonderful news first!"

"Oh, all right!" laughed her father. "Well,

then, how would you all like to go off on a trip?"

"A trip?" cried Bert. "A real trip? To Florida?"

"Well, hardly there again so soon," replied his father.

"Do you mean a trip to some city?" asked Nan.

"In a steamboat?" cried Freddie. "I want to go on a boat!"

"Yes, I think perhaps we can go on a boat," said Mr. Bobbsey.

"And in a train, too!" exclaimed Flossie. "I want to go on a train!"

"And I suppose, if we take this trip, we'll have to go on a train, also," and Mr. Bobbsey looked over the heads of the children and smiled at his wife who stood in the doorway.

"But you haven't told us yet where we are going," objected Nan.

"Is it to New York?" Bert wanted to know.

"Part of it is," his father replied.

"Oh, is it two trips?" Nan asked.

"Well, not exactly," answered Mr. Bobbsey. "You might say it has two parts to it, like a puzzle. The first part is to go on a trip to New York, and from there we'll go on a trip to——I'll let you see if you can guess. Come on, Bert, your turn first."

"To Uncle William's!" guessed Bert.

"No," answered his father. "Your turn, Nan."

"To Uncle Daniel's at Meadow Brook."

"No," and her father smiled at her.

"I know!" cried Freddie. "We're goin' on the houseboat."

"Wrong!" said Mr. Bobbsey. "Now what does my little fat fairy have to say?"

"Are we going swimming?" asked Flossie, who loved to splash in the water.

"Hardly!" laughed Daddy Bobbsey. "It's too cold. Well, none of you has guessed right, so I'll tell you. We're going to Washington to visit the Martin children who were here a while ago."

"Oh, to Washington!" cried Nan. "How nice!"

"And shall we see Billy and Nell?" Bert wanted to know.

"Yes," his father answered, "that's what

we'll do. I had a letter from Mr. Martin the
other day, inviting us all to come to his house
to pay him a visit," he went on. "I didn't know
just when I could go, but to-day I got another
letter from another man in Washington, saying he wanted to see me about some lumber
business. I may have to stay a week or two,
so I thought I would take the whole family
with me, and make a regular visit of it."

"Will you take us all?" asked Freddie.

"Yes."

"And Snap and Snoop an' an'——" began Flossie.

"Well, hardly the dog and the cat," explained her father. "Just mother, you four
twins and I will go to Washington."

"When can we start?" Nan asked.

"As soon as your mother can get you ready,"
replied Mr. Bobbsey.

"I'm ready now," announced Freddie.

"And shall we stop in New York?" Bert
demanded.

"Yes, for a day or so. And now what do
you think of my news?" asked Mr. Bobbsey.

"It's just—wonderful!" cried Nan. "Oh,

we'll have such fun with Nell and Billy!"

"And I want to see if I can drop a ball off Washington Monument," added Bert.

"Oh, you hadn't better try that," his father cautioned him. "You might hit some one. Well, then, it's all settled, and we'll go on the trip. How about it, Mother?" and he smiled at his wife.

"I think it will be very nice to go," she answered. "I like Mr. Martin and his children very much, and I'm sure we'll like Mrs. Martin too. It's fortunate that we can all go— that the children will not lose any schooling. For if all the classes stop, and the school is closed, they will all start evenly again when the boiler is fixed. So run along now, my twins, and get ready for lunch. Daddy and I have lots to talk about."

And so did the Bobbsey twins, as you can easily imagine.

If I told you all the things that happened in the next few days there would be but little else in this book except the story of getting ready for the journey. And as the trip itself is what you want to hear about, and especially what happened on it, I'll skip the getting ready and go right on with the story.

Trunks and valises were packed, Dinah and Sam were told what to do while the Bobbseys were away, and the children reminded the colored cook and her husband to be sure to feed Snap and Snoop plenty of things the dog and cat liked.

"Oh, I'll look after dem animiles all right, honey lamb!" said fat Dinah to Freddie. "I won't let 'em starve!"

"And maybe I can get another dog in Washington," said Freddie.

"And maybe I can find a cat!" added Flossie.

"Fo' de land sakes! doan brung any mo' catses an' dogses around heah," begged Dinah.

At last everything was in readiness. Mr. Bobbsey had written to Mr. Martin, telling of the coming of the Bobbsey twins to Washington, after a short stay in New York. The children said good-bye to Dinah and Sam, as well as to Snap and Snoop, and then one day they were taken to the railroad station in the automobile.

"All aboard!" cried the conductor, as the Bobbseys scrambled into the coach of the train that was to take them to New York. "All aboard!"

"Oh, isn't this fun?" cried Nan, as she settled herself in a seat with Bert.

"Great!" he agreed. "I wonder what will happen before we get back."

And it was going to be something very odd, I can tell you that much.

CHAPTER VIII

IN NEW YORK

THE Bobbsey twins had been to so many places, and had so often ridden in railroad trains, that this first part of their trip—journeying in the steam cars—was nothing new to them. They were quite like old travelers; at least Nan and Bert were. For Flossie and Freddie there was always sure to be something new and strange on such a long railroad trip.

The two older twins had picked out a nice seat in the center of the car, and were comfortably settled, Bert kindly letting Nan sit next to the window.

"You may sit here after a while," Nan said to Bert. "We'll take turns."

"That will be nice," replied Bert.

But Flossie and Freddie were not so easily pleased. Each of the smaller twins wanted to sit next to the window, and their father and mother knew that soon the little snub noses would be pressed close against the glass, and that the bright eyes would see everything that flashed by as the train speeded on.

But the trouble was that there were not enough seats for Flossie and Freddie each to have one, and, for a moment, it looked as though there would be a storm. Freddie slipped into the only whole vacant seat and took his place next the window.

"Oh, I want to sit there!" cried Flossie. "Mother, make Freddie give me that place! Please do!"

"No! I was first!" exclaimed the little boy, and this was true enough.

"I want to look out the window and see the cows!" went on Flossie, and her voice sounded as though she might cry at any moment. "I want to see the cows!"

"And I want to see the horses," declared Freddie. "If I'm going to be a fireman I've got to look at horses, haven't I?" he asked his father.

"Cows are better than horses!" half-sobbed

Flossie. "Mother, make Freddie let me sit where I can look out!"

"Children! Children! This isn't at all nice!" exclaimed Mrs. Bobbsey. "What shall I do?" she asked her husband in a low voice, for several of the passengers were looking at Flossie and Freddie, whose voices were rather loud.

"I'll let Flossie have my place," offered Nan. "I don't mind sitting in the outside seat. Here, Flossie, come over here and sit with Bert, and I'll sit with Freddie."

"Thank you, very much, Nan," said her mother in a low voice. "You are a good girl. I'm sure I don't know what makes Flossie and Freddie act so. They are usually pretty good on such a journey as this."

But Nan did not have to give up her place at the window, for a gentleman in the seat across the aisle arose and said to Mr. Bobbsey with a smile:

"Let your little girl take my seat near the window. I'm going into the smoking car, and I get off at the next station. I know how I liked to sit near a window, where I could see the horses and cows, when I was a little boy."

"Oh, thank you!" exclaimed Mr. Bobbsey. "That is very kind of you."

So the change was made. Flossie had a seat near one window, and Freddie near another, and Mr. Bobbsey sat with his "little fireman," while Mrs. Bobbsey took the other half of the seat with the "little fat fairy." Nan and Bert were together, and so there was peace at last. On rushed the train taking the Bobbsey twins to New York; and from there they were to go to Washington, where a strange adventure awaited them.

Nothing very much happened during the first part of the journey. Of course, Flossie and Freddie wanted many drinks of water, as they always did, and for a time they kept Bert busy going to the end of the car to fill the drinking cup. But as it was winter and the weather was not warm, the little twins did not want quite as much water as they would have wanted had the traveling been done on a hot day in summer. And at last Flossie and Freddie seemed to have had enough. They sat looking out of the window and speaking now and then of the many things they saw.

"I counted ten horses," announced Freddie after a while. "They were mostly on the road. I didn't see many horses in the fields."

"No, not very many horses are put out to graze in the fields in the winter, except perhaps on an extra warm day when there isn't any snow," said Mr. Bobbsey.

"And I saw two-sixteen cows!" exclaimed Flossie. "I saw them in a barnyard. Two-sixteen cows."

"There aren't so many cows as that; is there, Daddy?" asked Freddie.

"Well, perhaps not quite," agreed Mr. Bobbsey with a smile. "But Flossie saw a few cows, for I noticed them myself."

Then the smaller twins tried to count the telegraph poles and the trees that flashed past, and soon this made them rather drowsy. Flossie leaned back against her mother, and was soon sound asleep, while Freddie cuddled up in Daddy Bobbsey's arms and, in a little while, he, also, was in by-low land.

Bert and Nan took turns sitting next to the window, until the train boy came through with some magazines, and then the older twins were each allowed to buy one, and this kept them busy, looking at the pictures and reading the stories.

It was a rather long trip from Lakeport to New York, and it was evening when the train arrived in the big city. It was quite dark, and the smaller twins, at least, were tired and sleepy. But they roused up when they saw the crowds in the big station, and noticed the bright lights.

"I'm hungry, too!" exclaimed Freddie. "I want some supper. Oh, dear, I wish Dinah was here!"

"So do I!" added Flossie. "I guess my cat Snoop is having a good supper now."

"And I guess my dog Snap is, too!" went on Freddie. "Why can't we have supper?" he asked of his father, and several of the passengers, hurrying through the big station, turned to laugh at the chuby little fellow, who spoke very loud.

"We'll soon have supper, little fireman," said Mr. Bobbsey. "We might have eaten on the train, but I thought it best to wait until we reached our hotel, where we shall stay all night."

"How long are we going to be in New York?" asked Nan.

"Two or three days," her father replied. "I have some business to look after here. We may stay three days."

"That'll be fun!" exclaimed Bert. "There's a lot of things I want to see, and we didn't have time when we were here before."

The twins had been in New York before, as those of you know who have read the book called "The Bobbsey Twins In a Great City."

The hotel was soon reached, and, after being washed and freshened up in the bathroom of their apartment, the Bobbsey twins and their father and mother were ready to go down to supper. And not all the bright lights, nor the music which played all during the meal, could stop Flossie and Freddie from eating, nor Bert and Nan, either. The twins were very hungry.

The next day Mrs. Bobbsey took Nan and Flossie shopping with her, while Mr. Bobbsey took Bert and Freddie down town with him.

as the lumber merchant had to see some men on business, and he knew the two boys could wait in the different offices while he talked with his men friends.

"We will meet you in the Woolworth Building," said Mr. Bobbsey to his wife. "You bring Flossie and Nan there, and after we go up in the high tower we'll have lunch, and then go to the Bronx Park to see the animals."

"Oh, that will be fun!" cried Freddie. "I want to see a bear—two bears!"

"And I want to see ten-fifteen monkeys!" cried Flossie.

"Well, I hope you all get your wishes!" laughed Mother Bobbsey.

In one of the downtown offices where he had to stop to see a man, Mr. Bobbsey was kept rather a long time talking business, and Freddie and Bert got tired, or at least Freddie did. Bert was so interested in looking out of the high window at the crowds in the streets below, that he did not much care how long his father stayed. But Freddie wandered about the outer office, looking at the typewriter which a pretty girl was working so fast that. Bert said afterward, you could hardly see her fingers fly over the keys. The girl was too busy to pay much attention to what Freddie did until, all of a sudden, she looked down at the floor and exclaimed:

"Oh, it's raining in here! Or else a water pipe has burst!" She pointed to a little puddle of water that had formed under her desk, while another stream was running over the office floor.

"Why, it isn't raining!" declared Bert, for the sun was shining outside. "It can't be!"

"Then where did the water come from?" asked the girl.

"I—I guess I made it come!" confessed Freddie, walking out of a corner. "I got a drink from the water tank, but now I can't shut off the handle, and the water's comin' out as fast as anything!"

"Oh, my!" cried the girl, jumping up with a laugh, "I must shut it off before we have a flood here!"

"Freddie! what made you do it?" asked Bert.

"I couldn't help being thirsty, could I?" asked the little boy. "And it wasn't my fault the handle got stuck! I didn't know so much water would come out!"

And I suppose it really wasn't his fault. The girl soon shut off the water at the faucet, and a janitor mopped up the puddle on the floor, so that when Mr. Bobbsey came out with his friend from the inner office, everything was all right again. And the business man only laughed when he heard what Freddie had done.

"Now we'll go to the Woolworth Building," said Mr. Bobbsey to Freddie and Bert, as they went out on Broadway. "I think mother and the girls will be there waiting for us, as I stayed talking business longer than I meant to."

And, surely enough, Mrs. Bobbsey, Nan, and Flossie were waiting in the lobby of the big Woolworth Building when Mr. Bobbsey came up with the two boys. This building is the tallest one in the world used for business, and from the top of the golden tower one can look for miles and miles, across New York Bay, up toward the Bronx, over to Brooklyn and can see towns in New Jersey.

"We'll go up in the tower and have a view," said Mr. Bobbsey, "and then we'll get lunch and go to the Bronx, where the animals are."

They entered one of the many elevators, with a number of other persons who also wanted to go to the Woolworth tower, and, in a moment, the sliding doors were closed.

"Oh!" suddenly exclaimed Nan.

And Flossie, Freddie and Bert all said the same thing, while Mrs. Bobbsey clasped her husband's arm and looked rather queer.

"What's the matter?" asked her husband.

"Why, we're going up so fast!" exclaimed the children's mother. "It makes me feel queer!"

"This is an express elevator," said Mr. Bobbsey. "There are so many floors in this tall building that if an elevator went slowly, and stopped at each one, it would take too long to get to the top. So they have some express elevators, that start at the bottom floor, and don't stop until they get to floor thirty, or some such number as that."

"Are there thirty floors to this building?" asked Bert, as the elevator car, like a big cage in a tunnel standing on end, rushed up.

"Yes, and more," his father answered.

"I like to ride fast," said Freddie. "I wish we had an elevator like this at home."

They had to take another, and smaller elevator, that did not go so fast, to get to the very top of the tower, and from there the view was so wonderful that it almost took away the breath of the Bobbsey twins.

"My, this is high up!" exclaimed Bert, as he looked over the edge of the railing, and down at the people in the streets below, who seemed like ants crawling around.

"Well, I guess we'd better be going now," said Mr. Bobbsey, after a bit. "Come, children! Nan—Bert—Flossie—Why, where is Freddie?" he asked, looking around.

"Isn't he here?" cried Mrs. Bobbsey, her face turning white.

"I don't see him," went on Mr. Bobbsey. "He must have gone inside." But Freddie was not there, nor was he anywhere on the outside platform that surrounded the topmost peak of the tall building.

"Oh, where is he? What has happened to Freddie?" cried his mother. "If he has fallen! Freddie!"

CHAPTER IX

WASHINGTON AT LAST

THE startled cries of Mrs. Bobbsey alarmed a number of other women on the tower platform, and some one asked:

"Did your little boy fall off?"

"I don't know what happened to him!" said Mrs. Bobbsey, who was now almost crying. "He was here a moment ago, and now he's gone!"

"He couldn't have fallen off!" exclaimed Mr. Bobbsey. "Some one would have seen him. I think he must have gone down by himself in the little elevator. I'll ask the man."

The elevator, just then, was at the bottom of the tower, but it was soon on its way up, and Mrs. Bobbsey fairly rushed at the man as he opened the door.

"Where is my little boy? **Oh, have you seen my little boy?**" she cried.

95

"Well, I don't know, lady," answered the elevator man. "What sort of little boy was he?"

"He has blue eyes and light hair and——"

"Let me explain," Mr. Bobbsey spoke quietly. "My little boy, Freddie, was out on the tower platform with us looking at the view, a few minutes ago, and now we can't find him. We thought perhaps he slipped in here by himself and rode down with you."

"Well, he might have slipped into my elevator when I wasn't looking," answered the man. "I took two or three little boys down on the last load, but I didn't notice any one in particular. Better get in and ride to the ground floor. Maybe the superintendent or the head elevator man can tell you better than I. Get in and ride down with me."

"Oh, yes, and please hurry!" begged Mrs. Bobbsey. "Oh, what can have happened to Freddie?"

"I think you'll find him all right," said the elevator man. "No accident has happened or I'd have heard of it."

"Yes; don't worry!" advised Mr. Bobbsey.

But Mrs. Bobbsey could not help worrying, and Nan, Bert and Flossie were very much frightened. They were almost crying. Even though the Bobbseys got in an express elevator after getting out of the small, tower one, it could not go down fast enough to suit Freddie's mother. When the ground floor was reached she was the first to rush out.

One look around the big corridor of the Woolworth Building showed Mrs. Bobbsey that something had happened over near one of the elevators. There was a crowd there, and, for a moment, she was very much frightened. But the next second she saw Freddie himself, with a crowd of men around him, and they were all laughing.

"Oh, Freddie! where did you go and what have you been doing?" cried his frightened mother as she caught him up in her arms.

"I've been having rides in the elevator," announced the small boy. "And it went as fast as anything! I rode up and down lots of times!"

"Yes, that's what he did," said the elevator man, with a laugh. "I didn't pay much attention to him at first, but when I saw that he was staying in my car trip after trip, I asked him at what floor he wanted to get out. He said he didn't want to get out at all—that he liked me, and liked to stay in and ride!"

And at this the crowd laughed again.

"And is that what you have been doing, Freddie—riding up and down in the elevator?" asked Mr. Bobbsey.

"Yes, and I liked it!" exclaimed Freddie. "I wished Flossie was with me."

"I'm here now!" said the "little fat fairy," laughing. "I can ride with you now, Freddie."

"No! There has been enough of riding," said Mrs. Bobbsey. "And you gave me a bad fright, Freddie. Why did you wander away?"

" 'Cause I liked an elevator ride better than staying up so high where the wind blew," explained the little fellow.

And when they asked him more about it he said he had just slipped away from them while they were on the tower platform, gone back into the room and ridden down in the elevator with the other passengers. No one realized that Freddie was traveling all by himself, the elevator man thinking the blue-eyed and golden-haired boy was with a lady who had two other children by the hands.

Freddie rode to the ground floor, and then he just stayed in the express elevator, riding up and down and having a great time, until the second elevator man began to question him.

"Well, don't ever do it again," said Mr. Bobbsey, and Freddie promised that he would not.

After this there was a lunch, and then they all went up to Bronx Park, traveling in the subway, or the underground railway, which seems strange to so many visitors to New York. But the Bobbsey twins had traveled that way before, so they did not think it very odd.

"It's just like a big, long tunnel," said Bert, and so the subway is.

The Bronx Park is not such a nice place to visit in winter as it is in summer, but the children enjoyed it, and they spent some time in the elephant house, watching the big animals. There was also a hippopotamus there, and oh! what a big mouth he had. The keeper went in between the bars of the hippo's cage, with a pail full of bran mash, and cried:

"Open your mouth, boy!"

"Oh, look!" cried Bert.

And, as they looked, the hippopotamus opened his great, big red jaws as wide as he could, and the man just turned the whole pail full of soft bran into the hippo's mouth!

"Oh, what a big bite!" cried Freddie, and every one laughed.

"Does he always eat that way?" asked Mrs. Bobbsey of the keeper.

"Well, I generally feed him that way when there are visitors here," was the answer. "The children like to see the big red mouth open wide. And here's something else he does."

After the hippo, which is a short name for hippopotamus, had swallowed the pail full of bran mash, the keeper took up a loaf of bread from a box which seemed to have enough loaves in it for a small bakery, and cried: "Open again, old fellow!"

Wide open went the big mouth, and right into it the man tossed a whole loaf of bread. And the hippo closed his jaws and began chewing the whole loaf of bread as though it were only a single bite.

"Oh my!" cried Freddie and Flossie, and Freddie added: "If he came to a party you'd have to make an awful lot of sandwiches!"

"I should say so!" laughed the keeper. "One sandwich would hardly fill his hollow tooth, if he had one."

The children spent some little time in the Bronx Park, and enjoyed every moment. They liked to watch the funny monkeys, and see the buffaloes, which stayed outdoors even though it was quite cold.

The Bobbsey twins spent four days in New York, and every day was a delight to them. They had many other little adventures, but none quite so "scary" as the one where Freddie slipped away to ride in the elevator.

Finally, Mr. Bobbsey's business was finished, and one evening he said:

"To-morrow we go to Washington."

"Hurray!" exclaimed Bert. "Then I can see Billy Martin."

"And I can see Nell. I like her very much," added Nan.

"And I'm going to see the big monument!"
cried Freddie.

Early the next morning the Bobbsey family
took a train at the big Pennsylvania Station
to go to Washington. Nothing very strange
happened on that trip except that a lady in the
same car where the twins rode had a beautiful little white dog, and Flossie and Freddie
made friends with it at once, and had lots of
fun playing with the animal.

"Washington! Washington!" called the
trainman, after a ride of about five hours. "All
out for Washington!"

"Here at last, and I am glad of it," sighed
Mrs. Bobbsey. "I shall be glad to have supper
at the hotel and get to bed. I am tired!"

But the children did not seem to be tired.
They had enjoyed every moment of the trip.
In an automobile they rode to their hotel, and
soon were in their rooms, for Mr. Bobbsey
had engaged three with a nice bath. He had
decided it would be best to stay at a hotel
rather than at the Martins' house, because
there were so many Bobbseys; but they expected to visit their friends very often.

It was evening when the Bobbsey's arrived
in Washington, and too late to go sight-seeing. But on the way to the hotel in the automobile they had passed the Capitol, with the
wonderful lights showing on the dome, making
it look as though it had taken a bath in moon-
beams.

"Oh, it's just lovely here!" exclaimed Nan,
with a happy little sigh as they went down to
supper, or "dinner" as it is generally called,
even though it is eaten at night.

"Scrumptious!" agreed Bert.

The Bobbsey family had a little table all
to themselves at one side of the room, and a
waiter came up to serve them, Mr. Bobbsey
giving the order.

Nan and Bert and Flossie and Freddie
looked about. It was not the first time they
had stopped at a big hotel, but there was always something new and strange and interest-
ing to be seen.

Bert, who had been gazing about the room,
began to look at the dishes, knives and forks
the waiter was putting on the table. Suddenly
the dark-haired boy took hold of the sugar

bowl and turned it over, spilling out all the lumps.

"Why Bert! you shouldn't do that," exclaimed his father.

"I want to see what's on the bottom of this bowl," Bert said. "It looks just like the one Miss Pompret lost, and if it's the same I'll get a hundred dollars! Oh, look, it is the same! Nan, I've found her lost sugar bowl!" cried Bert.

CHAPTER X

LOST

Several persons, dining at different tables, looked over to the one where the Bobbseys were. They smiled as they heard Bert's excited voice and saw him with the empty, overturned sugar bowl in his hand.

"Yes, this is the very one Miss Pompret lost!" Bert went on. "If we can only find the milk pitcher now we'll have both pieces and we can get the reward. Look at the pitcher, Nan, and see if it's got the dog—I mean the lion—on as this has."

"Don't dare turn over the milk!" cried Mrs. Bobbsey, as Nan reached for the pitcher. "Spilling the sugar was bad enough. Bert, how could you?"

"But, Mother, that's the only way I could tell if it was Miss Pompret's!" said the boy, while Flossie and Freddie looked curiously at the heap of square lumps of sugar where Bert had emptied them in the middle of the table.

"Let me see that bowl, Bert," said Mr. Bobbsey a bit sternly. "I think you are making a big mistake. This isn't at all like the kind of china Miss Pompret has. Hers is much finer and thinner."

"But this has got a lion on the bottom, and it's in a circle just like the lion on Miss Pompret's dishes!" said Bert, as he passed the bowl to his father.

"Are the letters there—the letters 'J. W.'?" Nan asked eagerly.

"I don't see them," said Bert. "But the lion is there. Maybe the letters rubbed off, or maybe the tramp scratched 'em off."

"No, Bert," and Mr. Bobbsey shook his head, "this sugar bowl has a lion marked on the bottom, it is true, but it isn't the same kind that is on Miss Pompret's fine china. This tableware is made in Trenton, New Jersey, and it is new—it isn't as old as that Miss Pompret showed you. Now please pick up the sugar, and don't act so quickly again."

"Well, it looked just like her sugar bowl."

said Bert, as he began putting the square lumps back where they belonged. A smiling waiter saw what had happened, and came up with a sort of silver shovel, finishing what Bert had started to do.

"Wouldn't it have been great if we had really found her milk pitcher and sugar bowl?" asked Nan. "If we had the hundred dollars we could buy lots of things in Washington"

"Don't count on it," advised Mrs. Bobbsey. "You will probably never see or hear of Miss Pompret's missing china. But I'm glad Bert overturned the sugar bowl and not the milk pitcher searching for the lion mark."

"Oh, I wouldn't upset the milk!" exclaimed Bert with a laugh. "I knew the sugar wouldn't hurt the tablecloth."

So that incident passed, much to the amusement of the other hotel guests, and, really, no great harm was done, for the sugar was easily put back in the bowl. Then dinner was served, and for a time the Bobbsey twins did not talk very much. They were too busy with their knives, forks and spoons.

Bert wanted to go out and take a look at

the Capitol by night, to see the searchlights
that were arranged to cast their glow up on the
dome from the outside. Nan, also, said she
would like to take a little walk, and as Mrs.
Bobbsey was tired she said she would stay in
with Flossie and Freddie.

So it was arranged, and Mr. Bobbsey took
the two older children out of the hotel. It was
still early evening, and the streets were filled
with persons, some on foot, some in carriages,
and many in automobiles.

It was not far from the hotel where the
Bobbseys were staying to the Capitol, and soon
Bert and Nan, with their father, were standing in front of the beautiful structure, with its
long flight of broad steps leading up to the
main floor.

"It's just like the picture in my geography!"
exclaimed Nan, as she stood looking at it.

"But the picture in your book isn't lighted
up," objected Bert.

"Well, no," admitted Nan.

"The lights have not been in place very
long," explained Mr. Bobbsey. "Very likely
the picture in Nan's book was made before

some one thought of putting search lamps on the dome."

"Could we go inside?" Bert wanted to know. "I'd like to see where the President lives."

"He doesn't live in the Capitol," explained Nan. "He lives in the White House; doesn't he Daddy? Our history class had to learn that."

"Yes, the White House is the home of the President," said Mr. Bobbsey. "But we could go inside the Capitol for a few minutes I guess. The senators and congressmen are having a night session."

"What for?" asked Nan. "Do they have to work at night?"

"Sometimes."

"They don't work," declared Bert. "They just talk. I know, 'cause I heard Mr. Perkins say so down in our post-office at home one day. He said all the senators and congressmen did was talk and talk and talk!"

"Well, they do talk a lot!" laughed Bert's father. "But that is one of the ways in which they work. Now we'll go inside for a little while."

In spite of the fact that it was night the Capitol was a busy place. Later Mr. Bobbsey learned that the senators and congressmen were meeting at night in order to finish a lot of work so they could the sooner end the session—"adjourn," as it is called.

Bert and Nan walked around the tiled corridors. They saw men hurrying here and there, messenger boys rushing to and fro, and many visitors like themselves.

The children looked at the pictures and statues of the great men who had had a part in the making of United States history, but, naturally, Nan and Bert did not care very much for this.

"It isn't any fun!" exclaimed Bert. "Can't we go in and hear 'em talk and talk and talk, like Mr. Perkins said they did?"

"We'll go in and hear the senators and congressmen debate, or talk, as you call it, some other time," said Mr. Bobbsey. "We mustn't stay too late now on account of having left mother and Freddie and Flossie at the hotel. I think you've seen enough for the first evening."

So, after another little trip about the corridors, Bert and Nan followed their father outside and down the flight of broad steps.

"Say, this would be a great place to slide
down with a sled if there was any ice or
snow!" exclaimed Bert.

"They wouldn't let him, would they, Daddy?" asked Nan.

"Hardly," answered her father.

"Well, I can have fun some other way,"
Bert said. "I wish I could find Miss Pompret's dishes and get the hundred dollars."

"So do I!" sighed Nan.

But their father shook his head and told
them not to hope or think too much about such
a slim chance as that.

Flossie and Freddie were in bed and asleep
when Mr. Bobbsey and Bert and Nan reached
the hotel again, and, after a little talk with
their mother, telling her what they had seen,
the two older Bobbsey twins "turned in," as
Bert called it, having used this expression
when camping on Blueberry Island, and taking
the voyage on the deep, blue sea.

Because they were rather tired from their

trip, none of the Bobbseys arose very early the next morning.

"It's a real treat to me to be able to lie in bed one morning as long as I like," said Mrs. Bobbsey, with a happy sigh as Flossie crept in with her. "And I don't have to think whether or not Dinah will have breakfast on time. I'm having as much fun out of this trip as the children are," she told her husband.

"I am glad you are, my dear," he said. "I'll be able to go around with you a little to-day, but after that, for about a week, I shall be quite busy with Mr. Martin. But Mrs. Martin and Nell and Billy will go around with you and the children."

"When are we going to see Billy and Nell?" asked Bert, at the breakfast table.

"To-day," answered his father. "I telephoned Mr. Martin last night that we had arrived, and they expect us to lunch there to-day. But first I thought I'd take the children into the Congressional Library building. It is very wonderful and beautiful.

And it certainly was, as the children saw a little later, when their father led them up the broad steps. The library building was across a sort of park, or plaza, from the Capitol.

"We will just look around a little here, and then go on to Mr. Martin's," said Mr. Bobbsey. "It takes longer than an hour to see all the beautiful and wonderful pictures and statues here."

Mrs. Bobbsey was very much interested in the library, but I can not say as much for Flossie and Freddie, though Nan and Bert liked it. But the two smaller Bobbsey twins were anxious to get outdoors and "go somewhere."

"Well, we'll go now," said Mr. Bobbsey, when he and his wife had spent some little time admiring the decorations. "Come, Freddie. Where's Flossie?" he asked, as he looked around and did not see his "little fat fairy."

"She was here a little while ago," replied Nan. "I saw her with Freddie."

"Where did Flossie go, Freddie-boy?" asked his mother.

"Up there!" and the little chap pointed to a broad flight of stone steps.

"Oh, she has wandered away," said Mrs. Bobbsey.

"I'll run up and get her!" offered Mr. Bobbsey. Up the stairs he hurried, but he came back in a little while with a queer look on his face. "I can't find her," he said.

"Oh, Flossie's lost!" cried Freddie. "Oh, maybe she falled down stairs and got lost!"

CHAPTER XI

THE PRESIDENT

REALLY it was nothing new for one of the
Bobbsey twins to become lost—especially the
younger set, Flossie and Freddie. Some years
before, when they were younger, it had often
happened to Nan and Bert, but they were now
old enough, and large enough, to look after
themselves pretty well. But Flossie or Freddie, and sometimes both of them, were often
missing, especially when the family went to
some new place where there were strange ob-
jects to see, as was now the case in the Congressional Library.

"Where do you suppose Flossie could have
gone?" asked Mrs. Bobbsey, as she glanced
around the big rotunda in which they stood
with some other visitors who had come to the
city of Washington.

"I'll have to ask some of the men who are

n charge of this building," replied Daddy Bobbsey. "Are you sure you saw Flossie go up those stairs, Freddie?" he asked the little fireman.

"Well, she maybe went up, or she maybe went down," answered the boy. "I was lookin' at the pishures on the wall, and Flossie was by me. And then—well, she wasn't by me," he added, as if that explained it all. "But I saw a little girl go up the stairs and I thought maybe it was Flossie."

"But why didn't you tell mother, dear?" asked Mrs. Bobbsey. "If you had called to me when you saw Flossie going away I could have brought her back before she got lost. Why didn't you tell me that Flossie was going away?"

"'Cause," answered Freddie.

"Because why?" his father wanted to know

"'Cause I thought maybe Flossie wanted to slide down a banister of the stairs and maybe you wouldn't let her, and I wanted to see if she could slide down and then I could slide down too!"

"Well, that's a funny excuse!" exclaimed

Mr. Bobbsey. "I don't believe Flossie would slide down any banister here. But she has certainly wandered away, and we'll have to find her. You stay here with the children, so I'll know where to find you," Mr. Bobbsey said to his wife. "I'll go to look for Flossie."

"I want to come!" exclaimed Nan.

"No, you had better stay with mother," her father told her. "But I will take Bert along. He can take a message for me in case I have to send one. Come along!" he called to Nan's brother.

"All right, Daddy," answered Bert.

Up the big stone stairs went Daddy Bobbsey and Bert. Mrs. Bobbsey, with a worried look on her face, remained in the big rotunda with Nan and Freddie. The two children were worried too.

"Do you s'pose Flossie is hurt?" asked Nan.

"Oh, no, I don't believe so," and Mrs. Bobbsey tried to speak easily. "She has just gone into some room, or down some long hall, and lost her way, I think. You see there are so many rooms and halls in this building that it would be easy for even daddy or me to be lost. But your father will soon find Flossie and bring her back to us."

"But if they don't find her, Mamma?"

"Oh, they'll be sure to do that, Nan. There is nobody around this building who would hurt our little Flossie."

"What an awful big building it is," remarked Nan. "And just think of the thousands and thousands of books! Why, I didn't know there were so many books in the whole world! Mamma, do you suppose any of the people down here read all these books?"

"Hardly, Nan. They wouldn't have time enough to do that."

And now we shall see what happens to Mr. Bobbsey and Bert. Flossie's father decided to try upstairs first, as Freddie seemed to think that was the way his little sister had gone.

"Of course, he isn't very sure about it," said Mr. Bobbsey to Bert; "but we may as well start one way as the other. If she isn't upstairs she must be down. Now we'll look around and ask questions."

They did this, inquiring of every one they

met whether a little blue-eyed and flaxen-haired child had been seen wandering about. Some whom Mr. Bobbsey questioned were visitors, like himself, and others were men who worked in the big library. But, for a time, one and all gave the same answer; they had not seen Flossie.

Along the halls and into the different rooms went Mr. Bobbsey and Bert. But no Flossie could they find until, at last, they approached a very large room where a man with very white hair sat at a desk. The door of this room was open, and there were many books in cases around the walls.

"Excuse me," said Mr. Bobbsey to the elderly gentleman who looked up with a smile as Flossie's father and Bert entered the room. "Excuse me for disturbing you; but have you seen anything of a little girl——"

"Did she have blue eyes?" asked the old man.

"Yes!" eagerly answered Mr. Bobbsey.

"And did she have light hair?"

"Oh, yes! Have you seen her?"

Softly the man arose from his desk and

tiptoed over to a folding screen. He moved this to one side, and there, on a leather couch and covered by an office coat, was Flossie Bobbsey, fast asleep.

"Oh! Oh!" exclaimed Berf.

"Hush!" said the old man softly. "Don't awaken her. When she arouses I'll tell you how she came in here. It's quite a joke!"

"You stay here, Bert," said Mr. Bobbsey to his son, "and I'll go and get your mother, Nan and Freddie. I want them to see how cute Flossie looks. They'll be glad to know we have found her."

So while Bert sat in a chair in the old man's office Mr. Bobbsey hurried to tell his wife and the others the good news. And soon Mrs. Bobbsey and the rest of the children were peeping at Flossie as she lay asleep.

And then, suddenly, as they were all looking down at her, the little girl opened her eyes. She saw her mother and father; she saw Nan and Bert and Freddie; and then she looked at the kind old man with the white hair.

"Did you find a story book for me?" were the first words Flossie said.

"Well, I'm afraid not, my dear," was the old man's answer. "We don't have story books for little girls up here, though there may be some downstairs."

"Is that what she came in here for—a story book?" asked Mr. Bobbsey.

"I believe it was," answered the old man, with a smile. "I was busy at my desk when I heard the patter of little feet and a little girl's voice asking me for a story book. I looked around, and there stood your little one. I guessed, at once, that she must have wandered away from some visitors in the library, so I gave her a cake I happened to have in my lunch box, and got her to lie down on the sofa, as I saw she was tired. Then she fell asleep, and I covered her up and put the screen around her. I knew some one would come for her."

"Thank you, so much!" exclaimed Mrs. Bobbsey. "But, Flossie, how did you happen to come up here?"

"Oh, I wanted a story book," explained the little girl, as she sat up. "We have story books in our library, an' there ought to be story books here. I looked in this room an' I saw a lot

of books, so I did ask for one with a story in
it. I like a story about pigs an' bears an'—
an' everything!" finished Flossie.

"Well, I wish I had that kind of story book
for you, but I haven't!" laughed the old man.

"All my books are very dull, indeed, for
children, though when you grow up you may
like to read them," and he waved his hand at
the many books in the room.

So Flossie was lost and found again. The
old man was one of the librarians, and he had
taken good care of the little girl until her family came for her. After thanking him, Mr.
and Mrs. Bobbsey led their twins downstairs
and Mr. Bobbsey said:

"Well, I think we have have seen enough
of the library for a time. We had better go
and see the Martins."

"Oh, yes!" cried Bert. "Billy said he'd take
me to see the President."

"And I want to go, too!" added Nan.

"We'll see!" half promised her mother.

In an automobile the Bobbsey family rode
to where the Martin family lived. And you
can well believe that Billy and Nell were glad

to see the Bobbsey twins once more. Mrs.
Martin welcomed Mrs. Bobbsey, and soon
there was a happy reunion. Mr. Martin was
at his office, and Mr. Bobbsey said he would
go down there to see him.

"Then couldn't we go out and see the President while mother stays here and visits with
Mrs. Martin?" asked Nan. "Nell and Billy
will go with us."

"I think they might go," said Mrs. Martin.
"Billy and Nell know their way to the White
House very well, as they often go. It isn't
far from here."

"Well, I suppose they may go," said Mrs.
Bobbsey slowly.

"And I want to go, too!" exclaimed Freddie. "I want to see the dent."

"It isn't a *dent*—it's *President*—the head
of the United States!" explained Bert. "Our
teacher told us about him, and she said if ever
I came to Washington I ought to see the President."

"I want to see him too," cried Flossie.

"Let all the children go!" said Mrs. Martin. "I'll send one of my maids to walk along with them to make sure that they keep together. It is a nice day, and they may catch a glimpse of the President. He often goes for a drive from the White House around Washington about this time."

"Well, I suppose it will be a little treat for them," said Mrs. Bobbsey.

"Oh, goodie!" shouted Freddie.

So, a little later, the Bobbsey twins, with Nell and Billy Martin and one of the Martin maids, were walking toward the White House.

"There it is!" exclaimed Billy to Bert, as they turned the corner and came within view of the Executive Mansion, as it is often called.

"Oh, it *is* white!" cried Nan.

"Just like the pictures!" added Bert.

"It's got a big iron fence around," observed Freddie. "Is that so the President can't get out?"

"No, I guess it's so no unwanted people can get in," answered Nell.

The children and the maid walked down the street and looked through the iron fence into the big grounds, green even now though it was early winter. And in the midst of a great lawn stood the White House—the home of the President of the United States.

Suddenly two big iron gates were swung open. Several policemen began walking toward them from the lawn and some from the street outside.

"What's the matter?" asked Bert. "Is there a fire?"

"The President is coming out in his carriage," said Billy. "If we stand here we can see him! Look! Here comes the President!"

CHAPTER XII

WASHINGTON MONUMENT

Down the White House driveway rolled the
carriage, drawn by the prancing horses. It
was coming toward the iron gate near which,
on the sidewalk, stood the Bobbsey twins, with
their new friends, Billy and Nell Martin.

On the front seat of the carriage, which was
an open one, in spite of the fact that the day
was cool, though not very cold, sat two men.
One drove the horses and the other sat up very
straight and still.

"I should think he'd have an automobile,"
remarked Bert.

"He has," answered Billy. "He has an
auto—two of 'em, I guess. But lots of times
he rides around Washington in a carriage just
as he's doing now."

"That's right," chimed in Nell. "Sometimes we see the President and his wife in a
126

carriage, like now, and sometimes in a big auto."

"By this time the carriage, containing the President of the United States, was passing through the gate. A crowd of curious persons, who had seen what was going on, as had the Bobbsey twins, came hurrying up to catch a glimpse of the head of the nation. The police officers and the men from the White House ground kept the crowd from coming too close to the President's carriage.

The Chief Executive, as he is often called, saw the crowd of people waiting to watch him pass. Some of the ladies in the crowd waved their hands, and others their handkerchiefs, while the men raised their hats.

Billy put his hand to his cap, saluting as the soldiers do, and Bert, seeing this, did the same thing. Nell and Nan, being girls, were not, of course, expected to salute. As for Flossie and Freddie they were too small to do anything but just stare with all their eyes.

As the President's carriage drove along he smiled, bowed, and raised his hat to those who stood there to greet him. The President's wife also smiled and bowed. And then something in the eager faces of the Bobbsey twins and their friends, Nell and Billy, attracted the notice of the President's wife.

She smiled at the eager, happy-looking children, waved her hand to them, and spoke to her husband. He turned to look at the Bobbseys and their friends, and he waved his hand. He seemed to like to have the children watching him.

And then Flossie, with a quick little motion, kissed the tips of her chubby, rosy fingers and fluttered them eagerly toward the President's wife.

"I threw her a kiss!" exclaimed Flossie with a laugh.

"I'm goin' to throw one too," exclaimed Freddie. And he did.

The President's wife saw what the little Bobbsey twins had done, and, as quick as a flash, she kissed her hand back to Flossie and Freddie.

"Oh, isn't that sweet!" exclaimed a woman in the throng, and when, afterward, Nan told her mother what had happened, Mrs. Bobbsey said that when Flossie and Freddie grew up they would long remember their first sight of a President of the United States.

"Well, I guess that's all we can see now," remarked Billy, as the President's carriage rolled off down the street and the crowd that had gathered at the White House gate began moving on. The gates were closed, the policemen and guards turned away, and now the Bobbsey twins and their friends were ready for something else.

"Where do you want to go?" asked Billy of Bert.

"Oh, I don't know. 'Most anywhere, I guess."

"Could we go to see the Washington Monument?" asked Nan. "I've always wanted to see that, ever since I saw the picture of it in one of daddy's books at home."

"I don't believe we'd better go out there alone," said Nell. "It's quite a way from here. We'd better have our mothers or our fathers with us. But we can walk along the streets, and go in the big market, I guess."

"Let's do that!" agreed Billy. "There's

heaps of good things to eat in the market," he added to Bert. "It makes you hungry to go through it."

"Then I don't want to go!" laughed Bert. "I'm hungry now."

"I know where we can get some nice hot chocolate," said Nell. "It's in a drug store, and mother lets Billy and me go there sometimes when we have enough money from our allowance."

"Oh, I'm going to treat!" cried Bert. "I have fifty cents, and mother said I could spend it any way I pleased. Come on and we'll have chocolate. It's my treat!"

"We may go, mayn't we, Jane?" asked Nell, of the maid who had accompanied them.

"Oh, yes," was the smiling answer. "If you go to Payson's it will be all right."

And a little later six smiling, happy children, and a rosy, smiling maid were seated before a soda counter sipping sweet chocolate, and eating crisp crackers.

After that Billy and Nell took the Bobbsey twins to the market, which is really quite a wonderful place in Washington, and where, as Billy said, it really makes one hungry to see the many good things spread about and displayed on the stands.

"I think we've been gone long enough now," said the maid at last. "We had better go back."

So, after looking around a little longer at the part of the market where flowers were sold and where old negro women sold queer roots, barks, and herbs, the Bobbsey twins and their friends started slowly back toward the Martin house.

On the way they passed a store where china and glass dishes were sold, and there were many cups, saucers and plates in one of the windows.

"Wait a minute!" cried Bert, as Billy was about to pass on. "I want to look here!"

"What for?" Billy asked. "You don't need any dishes!"

"I want to see if Miss Pompret's sugar bowl and cream pitcher are here," Bert answered. "If Nan or I can find them we'll get a lot of money, and I could spend my part while I was here."

"Why Bert Bobbsey!" cried Nan, "you couldn't find Miss Pompret's things here—in a store like this. They only sell new china, and hers would be secondhand!"

"I know it," admitted Bert. "But there might be a sugar bowl and pitcher just like hers here, even if they were new."

"Oh, no!" exclaimed Nan. "There couldn't be any dishes like Miss Pompret's. She said there wasn't another set in this whole country."

"Well, I don't see 'em here, anyhow!" exclaimed Bert, after he had looked over the china in the window. "I guess her things will never be found."

"No, I guess not," agreed Billy, to whom, and his sister, Nan told the story of the reward of one hundred dollars offered by Miss Pompret for the return of her wonderful sugar bowl and cream pitcher, while Bert was looking at the window display.

"Well, did you have a good time?" asked Mrs. Bobbsey, when her twins came trooping back.

"Yes. And we saw the President!" cried Nan.

And then they told all about it.

The Bobbseys spent the rest of the day visiting their friends, the Martins, and returned to their hotel in the evening. They planned to have other pleasure going about the city to see the sights the next day and the day following.

"Could we ever go into the house where the President lives?" asked Nan of her father that night.

"Yes, we can visit the White House or, rather, one room in it," said Mr. Bobbsey. "What they call the 'East Room' is the one in which visitors are allowed. Perhaps we may go there to-morrow, if Mr. Martin and I can finish some business we are working on."

After breakfast the next morning the Bobbsey twins were glad to hear their father say that he would take them to the White House; and, a little later, in company with other visitors, they were allowed to enter the home of the President, and walk about the big room on the east side of the White House.

"I'm going to sit down on one of the chairs," said Nan. "Maybe it will be one that the President once sat on."

"Very likely it will be," laughed Mrs. Bobbsey, as Nan picked out a place into which she "wiggled." From the chair she smiled at her brothers and sister, and they, too, took turns sitting in the same chair.

Bert found a pin on the thick green carpet in the room. The carpet was almost as thick and green as the moss in the woods, and how Bert ever saw the tiny pin I don't know. But he had very sharp eyes.

"What are you going to do with it?" asked his father.

"Just keep it," the boy answered. "Maybe it's a pin the President's wife once used in her clothes."

"Oh, you think it's a souvenir!" laughed Mrs. Bobbsey, as Bert stuck the pin in the edge of his coat. And for a long time he kept that common, ordinary pin, and he used to show it to his boy friends, and tell them where he found it.

"The White House President's pin," he used to call it.

"And now," said Mr. Bobbsey, as they came from the White House, "I think we'll have time to see the Monument before lunch."

"That's good!" exclaimed Nan. "And shall we go up inside it?"

"I think so," her father replied.

Washington Monument, as a good many of you know, is not a solid shaft of stone. It is built of great granite blocks, as a building is built, and is, in fact, a building, for it has several little rooms in the base; rooms where men can stay who watch the big pointed shaft of stone, and other rooms where are kept the engines that run the elevator.

The bottom part of Washington Monument is square, and on one side is a doorway. Above the base the shaft itself stretches up over five hundred feet in height, and the top part is pointed, like the pyramids of the desert. The monument shaft is hollow, and there is a stairway inside, winding around the elevator shaft. Some people walk up the stairs to get to the top of the monument, where they can look out of small windows over the city of Washington and the Potomac River. But most persons prefer to go up and down in the elevator, though it is slow and, if there are many visitors they have to await their turns.

If the Bobbseys had walked up inside the monument they would have seen the stones contributed by the different states and territories. Each state sent on a certain kind of stone when the monument was being built, and these stones are built into the great shaft.

As it happened, there was not a very large crowd visiting the monument the day the Bobbseys were there, so they did not have long to wait for their turn in the elevator.

"This isn't fast like the Woolworth Building elevators were," remarked Bert, as they felt themselves being hoisted up.

"No," agreed his father. "But this does very well. This is not a business building, and there is no special hurry in getting to the top."

But at last they reached the end of their journey and stepped out of the elevator cage into a little room. There were windows on the sides, and from there the children could look out.

"It's awful high up," said Nan, as she peeped out.

"Not as high as the Woolworth Building,"

stated Bert, who had jotted down the figures in a little book he carried.

Flossie and Freddie had gone around to the other side of the elevator shaft with their mother, to look from the windows nearest the river, and, a moment later, Mr. Bobbsey, Nan and Bert heard a cry of:

"Oh, Flossie! Flossie! Look out! There it goes!"

CHAPTER XIII

A STRAY CAT

MR. BOBBSEY, who was standing near Bert and Nan, turned quickly as he heard his wife call and ran around to her side.

"What's the matter?" he called. "Has Flossie fallen?"

But one look was enough to show him that the two little Bobbsey twins and their mother were all right. But Flossie was without her hat, and she had been wearing a pretty one with little pink roses on it.

"What happened?" asked Mr. Bobbsey, while one of the men who stay inside the Monument at the top, to see that no accidents happen, came around to inquire if he could be of any help.

"It's Flossie's hat," explained Mrs. Bobbsey. "She was taking it off, as she said the rubber band hurt her, when a puff of wind came along——"

"And it just blowed my hat right away!"
cried Flossie. "It just blowed it right out of
my hand, and it went out of the window, my
hat did! And now I haven't any more hat,
and I'll—I'll—an'—an'—"

Flossie burst into tears.

"Never mind, little fat fairy!" her father
comforted her, as he put his arms around her.
"Daddy will get you another hat."

"But I want that one!" sobbed Flossie. "It
has such pretty roses on it, an' I liked 'em,
even if they didn't smell!"

"I guess the little girl's hat will be all right
when you get down on the ground," said the
monument man. "Many people lose their hats
up here, and unless it's a man's stiff one, or
unless it's raining or snowing, little harm
comes to them. I guess your little girl's hat
just fluttered to the ground like a bird, and
you can pick it up again."

"Do you think so?" asked Mrs. Bobbsey.

"Oh, you'll get her hat back again, ma'am,
I'm sure," the man said. "There's lots of boys
and young men who stay around the monument, hoping for a chance to earn a stray dime

or so by showing visitors around or carrying something. One of them probably saw the hat flutter out of the window, and somebody will pick it up."

"Well, let's go down and see," suggested Mr. Bobbsey. "I think we have had all the view we want."

"Don't cry, Flossie," whispered Nan consolingly, as she took her little sister by the hand. "We'll get your hat back again."

"And the roses, too?" Flossie asked.

"Yes, the roses and everything," her mother told her.

"If I were a big, grown-up fireman, I could climb down and get Flossie's hat," said Freddie. "That's what firemans do. They climb up and down big places and get things—and people," the little boy added after a moment of thought.

"Well, I don't want my little fireman climbing down Washington Monument," said Mr. Bobbsey. "It's safer to go down in the elevator."

And, a little later, the Bobbsey twins and their father and mother were back on the

ground again. Once outside the big stone
shaft, they saw a boy come running up with
Flossie's hat in his hand.

"Oh, look! Look!" cried the little girl.
"There it is! There it is!"

"Is this your hat?" the small boy wanted to
know. "I saw it blow out of the window, and
I chased it and chased it. I was afraid maybe
it would blow into the river."

"It was very nice of you," said Mr. Bobbsey,
and he gave the boy twenty-five cents, which
pleased that small chap very much.

Flossie's hat was a little dusty, but the pink
roses were not soiled, and soon she was wearing it again. Then, smiling and happy, she
was ready to go with the others to the next
sight-seeing place.

"Where now?" asked Bert, as they started
away from the little hill on which the Monument stands.

"I think we'll go to the Smithsonian Museum," said his father. "There are a few
things I want to see, though you children may
not be very much interested. Then I want to
take your mother to the art gallery and after

that—well, we'll see what happens next," and
he smiled at the Bobbsey twins.

"I know it will be something nice!" exclaimed Nan.

"I hope it's something good to eat!" murmured Bert. "I'm hungry!"

"I'd like to see a fire!" cried Freddie. "Do
they ever have fires in Washington, Daddy?"

"Oh, yes, big ones, sometimes. But we
really don't want to see any, because a fire
means danger and trouble for people."

"And wettings, too," put in Flossie. "Sometimes when Freddie plays fire he gets me wet."

"Well, I'm goin' to be a fireman when I
grow up," declared Freddie. "And I wish I
had my little fire engine now, 'cause I don't
like it not to have any fun."

"We'll have some fun this afternoon," his
father promised him.

Just as Mr. Bobbsey had expected, the children were not much amused in the art gallery or the museum. But Mrs. Bobbsey liked
these places, and, after all, as Nan said, they
wanted their mother to have a good time on
this Washington trip.

After lunch they went again to call on the Martins, as Mr. Bobbsey had to see the father of Billy and Nell on business.

"And where are we going to have some fun?" Bert asked, as they journeyed away from their hotel toward the Martin house.

"You'll see," his father promised. The children tried to guess what it might be, but they could not be sure of anything.

It did not take Mr. Bobbsey long to get tnrough with his business with Mr. Martin and then the father of the twins said to Mrs. Martin:

"Can you let Billy and Nell come with us on a little trip?"

"To be sure. But where are you going?" Mrs. Martin replied.

"I thought we'd take one of the big sightseeing autos and ride about the city, and perhaps outside a little way," said Mr. Bobbsey. "Nell and Billy can tell us the best way to go."

"Oh, yes! I can do that!" cried Billy. "I often take rides that way with my uncle when he comes to Washington. Come on, Nell! We'll get ready."

"May we really go?" asked Nell, of her mother.

"Yes, indeed!" was the answer.

So, a little later, the Bobbsey twins, with Billy and Nell and Mr. and Mrs. Bobbsey, were on one of the big automobiles. It was not too cold to ride outside, as they were all bundled up warm.

Through the different parts of the city the sight-seeing car went, a man on it telling the persons aboard about the different places of interest as they were passed. In a little while the machine rumbled out into the quieter streets, where the houses were rather far apart.

Then the automobile came to a stop, and some one asked:

"What's so wonderful to see here?"

"Nothing," the driver of the car answered. "But I have to get some water for the radiator. We won't be here very long. Those who want to, can get out and walk around."

"Yes, I'll be glad to stretch by legs," said one man with a laugh. He was sitting next to Mr. and Mrs. Bobbsey, and they began talking to him. Nan and Bert were talking to

Billy and Nell, and, for the time being, no one paid much attention to Flossie and Freddie, who were in a rear seat.

Suddenly Flossie called to her little brother:

"Oh, look! There's a cat! It's just like our Snoop!"

Freddie looked to where Flossie pointed with her chubby finger.

"No, that isn't like our Snoop," said the little boy, shaking his head.

"Yes, 'tis too!" declared his sister. "I'm going to get down and look at it. I like a cat, and I didn't see one close by for a long time."

"Neither did I," agreed Freddie. "If that one isn't like our Snoop, it's a nice cat, anyhow."

The cat, which seemed to be a stray one, was walking toward the car, its tail held high in the air "like a fishing pole."

Flossie and Freddie were in the rear seat, as I have said, and no one seemed to be paying any attention to them. Their father and mother were busy talking to the man who had gotten down to "stretch his legs," and Nan and Bert, with Billy and Nell, were busy talking.

"Let's get down," proposed Flossie.

"All right," agreed Freddie.

In another moment the two smaller Bobbsey twins had left their seat, climbed down the rear steps of the sight-seeing automobile, and were running toward the stray cat, which seemed to wait for them to come and pet it.

CHAPTER XIV

STRAY CHILDREN

"NICE pussy! Come and let me rub you!" said Freddie softly, as he held out his hand toward the stray cat.

"Yes, come here, Snoop!" added Flossie, as she walked along with her brother.

" 'Tisn't Snoop, and you mustn't call him that name," ordered Freddie.

"Well, he looks like Snoop," declared Flossie.

"But if that isn't his name he won't like to be called by it, no more than if I called you Susie when your name's Flossie," went on the little boy.

"Do you s'pose cats know their names?" asked Flossie.

"Course they do!" exclaimed her brother. "Don't our Snoop know his name when I call him, same as our dog Snap does?"

"Oh, well, but our cat is a very, very, smart cat!"

"Maybe this one is, too," Freddie said. "Anyhow, we'll just call him 'Puss' or 'Kittie,' and he'll like that, 'cause that's a name for any cat."

"That's so," agreed Flossie.

So calling to the stray cat in their soft, little voices, and holding out their hands to pet the animal, Flossie and Freddie walked farther away from the sight-seeing car, and soon they were petting the cat that, indeed, did look a bit like Snoop.

They stroked the soft back of the cat, rubbed its ears, and the animal rubbed up against their legs and purred. Then, suddenly, the cat heard a dog barking somewhere, and ran down toward the side entrance of a large, handsome house.

"Oh, come on!" cried Freddie to his sister, as he saw the cat running away. "Maybe there's some little cats back here, and we could get one to take home with us! Come on, Flossie!"

Flossie was willing enough to go, and in a

moment they were in the rear yard of one of the big houses, and out of sight from the street where the auto stood, while the man was putting water in the radiator.

The cat, once over its fright about the barking dog, seemed quieter now, and let the two little Bobbsey twins pet it again. Freddie saw a little box-like house in one corner of the yard and cried:

"I'm going to look here, Flossie! Maybe there's kittens in it!"

"Oh, let me see!" exclaimed the little girl. Forgetting, for a time, the stray cat they had started to pet, she and her brother ran over to the little box-like house.

"Better look out!" exclaimed Flossie, as they drew near.

"Why?" asked Freddie.

" 'Cause maybe there's a strange dog in that box."

"If there was a dog in this yard I guess this cat wouldn't have come in here," replied Freddie. "The cat ran when the other dog barked, and there can't be a dog here, else the cat wouldn't come in."

"I wonder what's there?" murmured Flossie.

"We'll soon find out," her brother said, as he bent over the little house, which was made of some boxes nailed together. There was a tiny window, with a piece of glass in it, and a small door.

Freddie began to open the little door, and he was not very much afraid, for now the cat was purring and rubbing around his legs, and the little boy felt sure that there could be no dog, or anything else scary, in the box-house, or else the cat would not have come so close.

"Maybe there isn't anything in there," suggested Flossie.

"Oh, there's got to be *something!*" declared Freddie. "It's a place for chickens, maybe."

"It's too little for chickens," said Flossie.

"Well, maybe it's a place for——"

That is as far as Freddie got in his talk, for, just then, a voice called from somewhere behind the children:

"Hi there! What do you want?"

"Oh!"

Freddie and Flossie both called out in surprise as they turned. They saw, standing on the back steps of the big house, a boy about as big as Bert.

"We came in after this cat," said Freddie, and he pointed to the stray pussy that was rubbing against his legs.

"Is it your cat?" the boy wanted to know.

Flossie shook her head.

"We just followed after him," she said. "He was out on the street, and we saw him, and we got down to rub him, and he heard a dog bark, and he ran in here, and we ran after him."

"Oh, I see," and the boy on the back steps smiled in a friendly way. "So it isn't your cat."

"No," answered Freddie, "Is it yours?"

The boy shook his head.

"I never saw the cat before," he answered. "It's a nice one, though, and maybe I'll keep it if you don't want it."

"Oh, we don't want it!" Freddie said quickly. "We have a cat of our own at home. His name is Snoop."

"And we have a dog, too," added Flossie. "But his name is Snap. And we have Dinah and Sam. Only they aren't a cat or a dog," she went on. "Dinah is our cook and Sam's her husband."

"Where do you live?" the boy asked.

"Oh, away off," explained Freddie. "We live in Lakeport, and we go to school."

"Only now there isn't any school," went on Flossie. "We can't have a fire 'cause something broke, and we came to Washington."

"Have you come here to live?" the strange boy questioned.

"No, only to visit," explained Freddie. "My father has to see Mr. Martin. Do you know Mr. Martin?"

The strange boy shook his head.

"I guess he doesn't live around here," he remarked. "I've lived here all my life; but there's nobody named Martin on this block. Where did you come from?"

"Offen the auto," explained Freddie. "We were riding on the auto with Billy Martin and Nell, and our father and mother and Nan and Bert and——"

"Say, there are a lot of you!" cried the boy with a laugh.

"It was a big auto," explained Flossie. "But the man had to stop and give it some water, so we got down to pet the cat. It's a nice cat."

"Yes, it's a nice cat all right," agreed the strange boy, and he came down the steps and began to rub the animal. "I like cats," he went on to the children. "What's your names?"

"Flossie and Freddie Bobbsey," answered Freddie. "What's yours?"

"Tom Walker," was the answer. "I guess I know where you came from. It's one of those big, sight-seeing autos. They often go through this street, but I never saw one stop before. You'd better look to see that it doesn't go off and leave you."

"Oh, the man said we could get down," returned Freddie. "And one man is going to stretch his legs. I'd like to see a man stretch his legs." he went on. "I wonder how far he can stretch them?"

"Not very far, I guess," remarked Tom Walker. "But I'm glad to see you, anyhow. I've been sick, and I had to stay home from

school, but I'm better now, and I'm going back
to-morrow. But I haven't had any one to play
with, and I'm glad you came in—you and the
cat."

"'Tisn't our cat!" Flossie hastily explained.

"Oh, I know!" agreed the boy. "But he
came in with you."

"We thought maybe there were kittens in
that box," and Freddie pointed to the one he
had been about to open.

"Oh, that was the place where I used to
keep my rabbits," said Tom. "I haven't any
now, but maybe I'll get some more; so I left
the little house in the yard. I like rabbits."

"So do I!" declared Freddie.

"And their nose goes sniff-snuff so funny!"
laughed Flossie. "Rabbits eat a lot of cab-
bage," she said. "If I had something to eat
now I would like it."

"Say, I can get some cookies!" cried Tom.
"Wait, I'll go in the house after some. You
wait here!"

"We'll wait!" said Freddie.

Into the house bounded Tom, and to the
cook in the kitchen he called:

"Oh, please give me some cookies. There's a stray cat in our yard and some stray children, and I want to give 'em something to eat, and——"

"My goodness, boy, how you do rattle on!" cried the cook. "What do you mean about stray cats and stray children?"

CHAPTER XV

"WHERE ARE THEY?"

FREDDIE and Flossie walked slowly up the yard, away from the empty rabbit house, and stood at the foot of the back steps up which Tom Walker had hurried to ask the cook for something to eat for the "stray children." The little Bobbsey twins had not heard what the cook said to Tom after he had asked for something to eat. But the cook repeated her question.

"What do you mean by stray cats and stray children?"

"There are the stray children out in the yard now," answered Tom. "They strayed away from some place, just as that dog I kept for a while once did. There was a stray cat, too, but I don't see it now."

"Stray children, is it?" cried the jolly cook. "Oh, look at the little darlin's!" she exclaimed, as she saw the small Bobbsey twins standing out in the yard, waiting for Tom to come back. Freddie and Flossie certainly did look very sweet and pretty with their new winter coats and caps on, though it was not very cold. It was not as cold in Washington as in Lakeport.

"Do you think he'll bring us anything to eat?" asked Freddie of Flossie, as they stood there waiting.

"I hope he does," the little girl answered "I'm hungry."

"So'm I!" Freddie admitted. "I guess that cat was, too. Where did he go?"

The cat answered himself, as though he knew he was being talked about. He came out from under the back steps, rubbed up against Flossie's fat, chubby legs with a mew and a purr, and then, seeing a place where the sun shone nice and warm on the steps, the cat curled up there and began to wash its face, using its paws as all cats do.

"Please, Sarah, can't I have something to eat for the stray children, and maybe for the cat?" again asked Tom of the cook.

"Oh, I dunno!" she answered. "Sure an' you're a bother! Your mother's out and I don't know what to do. These must be lost children, and, most likely, their father or mother's lookin' all over for 'em now. But I'd better bring 'em in an' keep 'em safe here, rather than let 'em wander about the streets. How did they come into our yard, do you think, Tom?"

"They just walked in, after the stray cat. They were on one of the big automobiles, and it stopped, so they got off. I told 'em maybe their folks would be looking for them," went on Tom, who was older than Flossie and Freddie. "But they seem to think it's all right."

"Well, they're lost, as sure as anything," declared the cook. "But it's best to keep 'em here until their folks can come after 'em. I'll give you something for them to eat, Tom, and then you must look after 'em, as I'm too busy, getting ready for the party your mother is going to have this night."

The kind cook soon got ready a plate of cookies and some glasses of milk for Flossie and Freddie. And, as Tom began to feel hungry himself when he saw something being made ready for his new little friends, a place was set for him, also, on a side table in the dining room.

"Call 'em in, now!" said the cook. "Everything is ready. And is the cat there?"

"Yes," answered Tom, as he looked out and saw the pussy curled up in the sun on the steps. "It's there."

"Well, I think I'll give it some milk," said the cook.

So, a little later, Flossie and Freddie, the stray children—for that is what they were—sat down to a nice little lunch in a strange house. Tom Walker sat down with them, and the stray cat had a saucer of milk in the kitchen.

"I looked out in the street," said the cook, as she came back to get Freddie another glass of milk, "but I don't see any automobile there. Did you really ride here in an auto?"

"Oh, yes," answered Freddie. "And the man on it all the time talked through a red horn, but I didn't know what he said."

"That was the man speaking through a

megaphone so everybody on the sight-seeing auto would know what they were looking at as they rode along," said Tom. "They often pass through here, though I haven't seen any to-day."

"But what to do about you children I don't know," said the cook, when Flossie and Freddie had eaten as much as they wanted. "If you did come here on an auto it's gone now, and there isn't a sign of it. I think you must have come two or three streets away from the car before you turned in here."

"Oh, no!" exclaimed Freddie. "When we got down off the auto we saw the cat and we came in after it. The auto was right out in front."

"Well, it isn't there now," said the cook. "I guess it must have gone away and taken your folks with it. Maybe they're looking for you. But I guess you'll have to stay here until they come to find you. You're too small to be allowed to go about alone."

"We like it here," said Flossie, settling back comfortably in her chair. "We can stay as long as you want us to."

"And we can stay to supper if you ask us," went on Freddie. "Course mother wouldn't let us ask for an invitation, but if you *want* to ask us to stay we can't help it."

" 'Specially if you have cake," added Flossie, smoothing out her dress.

"Yes, 'specially cake!" agreed Freddie.

"Oh my!" laughed the cook. "Sure an' you're very funny! But I like you. And I only wish I knew where your folks were. But the best I can do is to keep you here until they come. They must know about where they lost you. Come, Tom, take the stray children out and amuse them. Your mother'll be home pretty soon."

If Tom's mother had been at home she would have at once telephoned and told the police that she had two lost—or stray—children at her house, so that in case Mr. and Mrs. Bobbsey inquired, as they did, they would know that the tots were all right.

But Mrs. Walker was not at home, and the cook did the best she could. She made sure the children were safe and comfortable while they were with her.

And, after they had eaten, Tom got out some of his toys, and he and Flossie and Freddie had a good time playing about the house and in the yard. The stray cat wandered away while Flossie and Freddie were eating their little lunch, and the Bobbsey twins did not see him again.

Now while Flossie and Freddie were having a pretty good time, eating cookies and drinking milk, there was much excitement on the big sight-seeing car where Mr. and Mrs. Bobbsey, Nan, Bert, and the other, still had their seats.

For some little time after the car had stopped to allow the man to put water in the radiator, neither Mr. nor Mrs. Bobbsey missed their smaller twins. They were busy talking, and Bert and Nan were looking about and having a good time, talking to Billy and Nell Martin.

At last, however, the auto man called: "Everything is all right! Get on board!"

That meant he was going to start off again, and it was not until then that Mrs. Bobbsey thought to look around to see if Flossie and

Freddie were all right. And, of course, she did not see them.

"Flossie! Freddie! Where are you?" called Mrs. Bobbsey.

There was no answer, and the seat which the two smaller children had been in on the big bus, was empty.

"Oh, Daddy!" cried Mrs. Bobbsey, "Flossie and Freddie have gone."

"Gone? Gone where?" Mr. Bobbsey asked.

"That's it—I can't say," answered Mrs. Bobbsey. "The last I saw of them was when the auto stopped."

"I saw the two little tots climb down off the rear steps of the car," said the man who had wanted to "stretch his legs." "They seemed to be going after something," he added.

"It was a cat," said the woman next to the big man who had last spoken. "I saw the children get down and go toward a stray cat and then I got to thinking of something else."

"Oh, if it was a cat you might know it!" exclaimed Mrs. Bobbsey with a laugh. "I guess they're all right. They can't have gone far. Probably they are on the other side of the street, looking at some bedraggled kitten."

But a look up and down the street did not show Flossie and Freddie. By this time the auto was all ready to start off again.

"But we can't go without Flossie and Freddie!" cried Nan.

"I should say not!" exclaimed Mrs. Bobbsey. "Oh, where are they? Where can my darlings have gone? What has happened?"

CHAPTER XVI

THE FIRE BELL

MRS. BOBBSEY's cries of alarm, of course, excited all the other passengers who had got back on the sight-seeing auto, ready to start off again. They had had a little rest while the water was being put into the radiator, and the man had "stretched his legs" all he wanted to, it seemed.

"The children can't be far away," said Mr. Bobbsey. "They were here only a moment ago. Even if they have wandered off, which is probably what they have done, they can't be far."

"They're all right," the man who drove the car assured Mr. Bobbsey. "I didn't see 'em go away, of course, as I was busy, but I'm sure nothing has happened."

"But what shall we do?" cried Mrs. Bobbsey, and tears came into her eyes. "It does

165

seem as if more things have happened to Flossie and Freddie since we started on this trip than ever before."

"Oh, they'll be all right," declared Mr. Bobbsey. "I'll look around. Perhaps they may have gone into one of these houses."

"Did you look under the seats?" asked Bert.

"Under the seats!" exclaimed Billy. "What good would that do? Your brother and sister couldn't be under there!"

"Pooh, you don't know much about Flossie and Freddie!" answered Bert. "They can be in more places than you can think of; can't they, Nan?"

"Yes, they do get into queer places sometimes. But they aren't under my seat," and Nan looked, to make sure.

"Nor mine," added Nell, as she looked also.

Some of the other passengers on the auto did the same thing. Mr. Bobbsey really thought it might be possible that Freddie and Flossie, for some queer reason, might have crawled under one of the seats when the big machine stopped for water. But the children were not there.

"Oh, what shall we do?" exclaimed Mrs. Bobbsey.

"They'll be all right," her husband answered. "They can't be far away."

"That's right ma'am," said a fat, jolly-looking man.

"Some of you go and inquire in the houses near here," suggested the man who drove the auto. "And I'll go and telephone back to the office, and see if they're there."

"But how could they be at your automobile office?" Mrs. Bobbsey wanted to know.

"It might easily happen," replied the man. "We run a number of these big machines. One of them may have passed out this way while I was stopping here for water, and perhaps none of us notice it, and the children may have climbed on and gone on that car, thinking it was this one."

"They couldn't get on if the auto didn't stop," said Billy.

"Well, maybe it stopped," returned the driver. "Perhaps it passed up the next street. The children may have gone down there and gotten on. Whatever has happened, your little ones are all right, ma'am; I'm sure of that."

"I wish I could be!" sighed Mrs. Bobbsey.

Several men volunteered to help Mr. Bobbsey look for the missing twins, and they went to the doors of nearby houses and rang the bells. But to all the answer was the same. Flossie and Freddie had not been seen.

And the reason for this was that the small Bobbsey twins, in following the stray cat, had turned a corner and gone down another street, and were on the block next the one where the auto stood. That was the reason the Walker cook, looking out in front, could see no machine, and why it was that none of those who helped Mr. Bobbsey look for the missing children could find them.

"Well, this is certainly queer!" exclaimed Mr. Bobbsey, when at none of the houses was there any word of Flossie and Freddie.

"But what are we to do?" cried his wife.

"I think we'd better notify the police," said Mr. Bobbsey. "That will be the surest way."

"Yes, I think it will," agreed the auto man. "I telephoned to the office, but they said no lost children had been turned in. Get aboard, every one, and I'll drive to the nearest police station."

Away started the big auto, leaving Flossie and Freddie behind in the home of Tom Walker on the next street. And though Mr. and Mrs. Bobbsey, with Nan and Bert and Billy and Nell were much worried, Flossie and Freddie themselves, were having a good time.

For they were playing with Tom, who showed them his toys, and he told them about the rabbits he used to keep.

"I have had as many as six big ones at a time," Tom said. "And I had one pair that had the finest red eyes you ever saw."

"Red eyes!" cried Flossie. "What funny rabbits they must have been!"

"Oh, I know some rabbits have red eyes," declared Freddie. "But not very many. Bert said so."

"I don't believe I'd like to have red eyes," answered his twin sister. "Everybody'd think I'd been crying."

"They're not red that way," explained Tom. "They just have the color red in them; just as some people have black eyes, blue eyes, and brown eyes—like that."

"Oh! Say, I heard Nan say once that a girl in her room at school had one black eye and one grey eye. Wasn't that funny?"

"It certainly was," answered Tom. And then he showed the little Bobbsey twins a number of picture books and a locomotive which went around a little track.

Freddie and Flossie were having such a good time that they never thought their father and mother might be worried about them.

But, after a while, Mrs. Walker came home. You can well imagine how surprised she was when she found the two lost, strayed children in her house.

"And so they got off one of the sight-seeing autos, did they?" cried Tom's mother. "Oh, my dears! I'm glad you're here, of course, and glad you had a good time with Tom. But your mother and father will be much frightened! I must telephone to the police at once."

"We'll not be arrested, shall we?" asked Freddie anxiously.

"No, indeed, my dear! Of course not! But your parents have probably already telephoned the police, who must be looking for you. I'll let them know I have you safe."

"Why, course we're safe!" cried Flossie.

So Mrs. Walker telephoned. And, just as she guessed, the police were already preparing to start out to hunt for the missing children. But as soon as they got Mrs. Walker's message everything was all right.

"They're found!" cried Mr. Bobbsey to his wife, when a police officer telephoned to the hotel to let the father of the small Bobbsey twins know that the children were safe. "They're all right!"

"Where were they?" asked his wife.

"All the while they were right around the corner and just in the next street from where our auto was standing."

"Oh, dear me!" cried Mrs. Bobbsey, "what a relief."

"I should say so!" agreed Mrs. Martin, who had gone to the hotel, where her friends were staying, to do what she could to help them.

"I'll get a taxicab and bring them straight here," said Mr. Bobbsey.

A little later Flossie and Freddie were back "home" again. That is, if you call a hotel "home," and it was, for the time, to the traveling Bobbseys.

"What made you do it?" asked Flossie's mother, when the story had been told. "What made you go after the stray cat?"

"It was such a nice cat!" said the little girl.

"And we wanted to see if it was like our Snoop," added Freddie.

"Well, don't do such a thing again!" ordered Mr. Bobbsey.

"No, we won't!" promised Freddie.

"No, but they'll do something worse," said Bert in a low voice to his friend Billy, who had also come to the hotel.

So the little excitement was over, and soon the Bobbsey twins were in bed. Not, however, before Nan had asked her father:

"Where are you going to take us to-morrow?"

"To Mount Vernon, I think," was his answer.

"Oh, where Washington used to live!" remarked Bert.

"Where——" But right there Freddie went
to sleep.

"Yes, and where he is buried," added Nan.
And then she, too, fell asleep. And she
dreamed that Flossie and Freddie were lost
again, and that she started out to find them
riding on the back of a big cat while Bert
rode on a dog, like Snap.

"And I was so glad when I woke up and
found it was only a dream," said Nan, telling
Nell about it afterward.

There are two ways of going to Mount
Vernon from the city of Washington. Mount
Vernon is down on the Potomac River, and
one may travel to it by means of a small
steamer, which makes excursion trips, or one
can get there in a trolley car.

"I think we'll go down by boat and come
back by trolley," said Mr. Bobbsey. "In that
way we can see more."

"I'd rather go on the boat all the while,"
said Freddie. "Maybe I could be a fireman
on the boat."

"Oh, I think they have all the firemen they need,' laughed his father.

"Is Mount Vernon an old place?" asked Nan. as they were getting ready to leave their hotel after breakfast.

"Quite old, yes," her father answered.

"And do they have old-fashioned things there, like spinning wheels, and old guns and things like those in Washington's headquarters that we went to once?" Nan went on.

"Why, yes, perhaps they do," her father said. "Why do you ask?"

"Oh, I was just thinking," went on Nan, "that if they had a lot of old-fashioned things there they might have Miss Pompret's sugar bowl and cream pitcher, and we could get 'em for her."

"How could we?" asked Bert. "If they were there they'd belong to Washington, wouldn't they, Daddy?"

"Well, I suppose all the things in the house once belonged to him or his friends," said Mr. Bobbsey. "But I don't imagine those two missing pieces of Miss Pompret's set will be at Mount Vernon, Nan."

"No, I don't s'pose so," sighed the little girl. "But, oh, I would like to find 'em!"

"And get the hundred dollars reward!" added Bert.

"Don't think too much of that," advised their mother. "Of course it would be nice to find Miss Pompret's dishes, and do her a favor, but I think it is out of the question after all these years that they have been lost."

The weather was colder than on the day before, when Flossie and Freddie had been lost, and the sun shone fitfully from behind clouds.

"I think we are going to have a snow storm," said Mr. Bobbsey, on their way to take the boat for Mt. Vernon.

"Oh, goodie!" cried Flossie. "I hope it snows a lot!"

"So do I!" added Freddie. "Could we send home for our sled if there's lots of snow, Daddy?" he asked.

"I hardly think it would be worth while," said his father. "We are not going to be here much more than a week longer. And it would be quite a lot of work to get your sleds here and send them home again. I think you'll get all the coasting and skating you want when we get back to Lakeport."

"Anyway, we're having a nice time while we're here," said Nan, with a happy little sigh.

"It's fun when Freddie and Flossie don't get lost," added Bert. "I'm going to keep watch of 'em this time."

"I'll help," added Nan. "Oh, here are Billy and Nell!" she called, waving her hand to their new friends. The Martin children were to go to Mount Vernon with the Bobbsey twins, and they now met them near the place from which the boat started.

"All aboard!" cried Freddie, as they went on the small steamer that was to take them to Mount Vernon. "All aboard. I'm the fire-man!"

"There aren't any fires to put out," said Nell, teasing the small chap a little.

"Yes, there is—a fire in the boiler, and it makes steam," said Freddie, who had often looked in the engine room of steamers. "But I'm not that kind of fireman. I put out fires.

I'm going to be a real fireman when I grow up," he added.

Soon they were comfortably seated on board the boat, which after a bit moved out into the Potomac. Mr. and Mrs. Bobbsey were talking together. Nan, Bert, Billy and Nell were watching another boat which was passing, and Flossie was near them. But Freddie had slipped away, in spite of what Bert had said about going to keep a watchful eye on his small brother.

Suddenly, when the steamer was well out in the river, there was the loud clanging of a bell, and a voice cried:

"Fire! Fire! Fire!"

At once every one on the boat jumped up. The women looked frightened, while the men seemed uncertain what to do.

"Clang! Clang! Clang!" rang the fire alarm bell.

CHAPTER XVII

FREDDIE'S REAL ALARM

"I HOPE nothing has happened—that the boat isn't on fire," said Mrs. Bobbsey to her husband. "That would be terrible!"

"I hardly think that is it," he said. "There may be a small fire, somewhere on the boat, but, even if there is, they have a way of putting it out. I'll go and see what it is. You stay with the children."

But just then, after another clanging of the bell, some one was heard to laugh—the ringing, hearty laugh of a man.

"There!" exclaimed Mr. Bobbsey, "I guess everything is all right. They wouldn't be laughing if there was any danger."

"Let's go to the fire!" cried Bert. "I want to see it!"

"So do I!" chimed in his new chum, Billy, eagerly.

178

"Oh, can't we see it; whatever it is?" begged Nan.

"First I'll have to make sure there is a fire," replied Mr. Bobbsey. "I hope there isn't. But, if there should be a small one, and the firemen on the boat are putting it out, and if they let us get near enough to see, and if the smoke isn't too thick——"

"Oh, Daddy! Not so many 'ifs,' please!" laughed Nan.

The Bobbseys all laughed at this, as did Nell and Billy.

"Freddie would like to see the fire, if there is one," remarked Nell Martin.

"Oh, that's so! Where is Freddie?" cried Bert.

Then, for the first time, Mr. and Mrs. Bobbsey noticed that the little blue-eyed and light-haired boy was not with them.

But at that moment around the corner of a deck cabin came a man wearing a cap with gold braid around the edge. He was smiling and leading by the hand a little boy. And the little boy was Freddie!

"Oh, there he is!" cried Flossie. "Freddie,

where were you?" she asked. "And did you been to see the fire?"

"Well, I rather guess he did!" exclaimed the man, who was the captain of the boat. "He was the whole fire himself!"

"The whole fire?" cried Mr. Bobbsey. "Do you mean to say that my little boy started a fire?"

"Oh, nothing as bad as that!" said the captain, and he smiled down on Freddie who smiled up at him in return. "No, all your little boy did was to ring the fire alarm bell and then call out 'Fire!' But of course that was enough to start things going, and we had quite a good deal of excitement for a time. But it's all right now, and I think he won't do it again."

"Just what did he do?" asked Mrs. Bobbsey, as Freddie came over to stand beside his mother. He looked rather ashamed.

"Well, on the deck, back of the wheel-house, which is the little place where I or my men stand to steer the boat, there is a fire alarm bell. It's there for any one to ring who finds the boat on fire, and when the bell is rung all

my firemen hurry to put out the blaze," said
the captain.

"Now this little chap of yours went up and
rang that bell, and then he cried out 'Fire,' as
I've told you. Then—well, lots of things happened. But I couldn't help laughing when I
found out it was a false alarm, and learned
just why Freddie, as he tells me his name is,
rang the bell."

"And why was that?" asked Mr. Bobbsey,
quickly.

Freddie spoke up for himself.

"The bell had a sign on it," said the little
fellow, "and it said to ring it for a fire. I
wanted to see a fire, and so I rang the bell
and—and——"

Freddie's lips began to quiver. He was just
ready to cry.

"There, there, my little man!" said the captain kindly. "No harm is done. Don't worry.
It's all right," and he patted Freddie on the
shoulder.

"You see it's just as Freddie says," the captain went on. "There is a large sign painted
near the bell which reads: 'Ring this for a

fire.' I suppose it would be better to say: 'Ring the bell in case of fire.' I believe I'll have it changed to read that way. Anyhow, your little boy saw the sign over the bell. And on the bell is a rope so low that any one, even a child, can reach it. So your Freddie just pulled the rope, clanged the bell, and then he cried 'Fire!' as loudly as he could. Some one else took up the cry, and, there you are!'

"And so you rang the bell, did you, Freddie, because you wanted to see a fire?" asked the father of the little fellow.

"Yes," answered Flossie's brother. "I wanted to see how they put out a fire on a boat, and the bell said for to ring for a fire, and I wanted a fire, I did; not a big one, just a little one, and so——"

"And so you just naturally rang the bell!" laughed the captain. "Well, I guess that's partly my fault for having the sign read that way. I'll have it changed. But your little boy is quite smart to be able to read so well," he added.

"Oh, I go to school!" said Freddie proudly, "only there isn't any now on account of—well

I guess the boiler got on fire," he added.

"He's a regular little fireman," said Mr. Bobbsey. "He can't read very much, but one of the first words he learned to spell was 'fire,' and he's never forgotten it."

The boat was now going on down the river toward Mount Vernon, and the excitement caused by the false alarm of fire was over.

Of course Freddie had done wrong, though he had not meant to, and perhaps it was not all his fault. However, his father and mother scolded him a little, and he promised never to do such a thing again.

I wish I could tell you that the Bobbsey twins were interested in Mount Vernon, but the truth of the matter is that the two younger ones were so busy talking about Freddie's fire alarm, and Bert and Nan, with Billy and Nell, also laughed so much about it, that they did not pay much attention to the tomb of the great Washington, or anything about the place where the first President of the United States once had his home.

Of course Mr. and Mrs. Bobbsey were interested in the place where the wonderful man

had lived, and they looked about the grounds
where he had once walked, and they visited
the house where he had lived. But, really, the
children did not care much for it.

"When are we going back?" asked Freddie
several times.

"Don't you like it here?" asked his mother.
"Just think of what a wonderful and beautiful
place this is!"

"Well," said Freddie slowly, "I didn't see
any fire engines yet."

Mrs. Bobbsey tried not to laugh, but it was
hard work.

"I think we'd better go back to Washington," she said to her husband.

"I think so, too," he answered, and back to
Washington they went. This time they rode
on a trolley car, and there was no danger of
Freddie's sending in an alarm of fire.

And on the way home something quite wonderful happened. At least it was wonderful
for Freddie.

He was looking out of the window, when
suddenly he gave a yell that startled his father
and mother, as well as Nan, Bert, Nell and

Flossie, and that made the other passengers sit up.

"Oh, look! There's a fire engine! There's a fire engine!" cried the little chap, pointing; and, surely enough, there was one going along the street. It was bright and shiny, smoke was pouring from it and the horses were prancing.

The other Bobbsey twins turned to look at it, and Bert said:

"Pooh, that's only coming back from an alarm."

"That's so," agreed Mr. Bobbsey. "The horses are going too slowly to be running to a fire, Freddie. They must be coming back."

"Well, it's a fire engine, anyhow," said Freddie, and every one had to agree with him. Freddie watched the shiny engine until it was out of sight, and then he talked about nothing else but fires on the way home.

Tired, but well satisfied with their trip, the Bobbsey's reached their hotel, and the Martin children went to their home, promising to meet the following day and see more Washington sights

It was about the middle of the night that Mrs. Bobbsey, who slept in the same room with Flossie and Freddie, felt herself being shaken in bed. She roused up to see, in the dim light, Freddie standing near her, and shaking her with his chubby hands.

"What is it, dear?" asked Mrs. Bobbsey, sleepily.

"Fire!" hoarsely whispered Freddie. "The house is on fire, and it's real, too, this time!"

CHAPTER XVIII

THE ORIENTAL CHILDREN

AT first Mrs. Bobbsey was too sleepy, from having been so quickly awakened, to really understand what Freddie was saying. She turned over in bed, so as to get a better look at the small boy, who was in his night gown, and with his hair all tousled and frowsled from the pillow. There was no mistake about it—Mrs. Bobbsey was not dreaming. Her little boy was really standing beside her and shaking her. And once more he said:

"Wake up, Momsie! There's a real fire! This house is on fire, and we've got to get out. I can hear the fire engines!"

"Oh, Freddie! you're walking in your sleep again," said his mother as she sat up, now quite awake. "You have been dreaming, and you're walking in your sleep!"

Freddie had done this once or twice before.

thought not since he had come to Washington.

"The excitement of going to Mount Vernon, and your ringing of the fire bell on the boat has made you dream of a fire, Freddie," his mother went on. "It isn't real. There isn't any fire in this hotel, nor near here. Go back to sleep."

"But, Momsie, I'm awake now!" cried Freddie. "And the fire is real! I can see the red light and I can hear the engine puffin'! Look, you can see the light!"

Freddie pointed to a window near his mother's bed. And, as she looked, she certainly saw a red, flickering light. And then she heard the whistle which she knew came from a fire engine. It was not like a locomotive whistle, and, besides, there were no trains near the hotel!

"Oh, it is a fire!" cried Mrs. Bobbsey. "Freddie, call your father!"

Mr. Bobbsey slept in the next room with Bert, while Nan had a little bed chamber next to her mother's, on the other side of the bath room.

But there was no need to call Mr. Bobbsey.

In his big, warm bath robe he now came stalking into his wife's room.

"Don't be frightened," he said. "There's a small fire in the building next to this hotel. But it is almost out, and there is no danger. Stay right in bed."

"But it's a real fire, isn't it, Daddy?" cried Freddie. "I heard the engines puffin', and I saw the red light and it woke me up and I comed in and told Momsie; and it's a real fire, isn't it?"

"Yes, Freddie, it's a real fire all right," said Mr. Bobbsey. "But don't talk so loud, nor get excited. You may awaken the people in the other rooms around us, and there is no need. I was talking to the night clerk of the hotel over the telephone from my room, and he says there is no danger. There is a big brick wall between our hotel and the place next door, which is on fire. The blaze can't get through that."

"Can't I look out the window and see the engines?" Freddie wanted to know.

"Yes, I guess it would be too bad not to let you see them, as long as they are here, and it's a real fire," answered Mrs. Bobbsey. "I hope no one was hurt next door," she added to her husband.

"I think not," he replied. "The fire is only a small one. It is almost out."

So Freddie had his dearest wish come true in the middle of the night—he saw some real fire engines puffing away, spouting sparks and smoke, and pumping water on a real fire. Of course the little boy could not see the water spurting from the hose, as that was happening inside the burning building. But Freddie could see some of the firemen at work, and he could see the engines shining in the light from the fire and the glare of the electric lamps. So he was satisfied.

Bert and Nan were awakened, and they, too, looked out on the night scene. They were glad it was not their hotel which was on fire. As for Flossie, she slept so soundly that she never knew a thing about it until the next morning. And then when Freddie told her, and talked about it at the breakfast table, Flossie said:

"I don't care! I think you're real mean, Freddy Bobbsey, to have a fire all to yourself!"

"Oh, my dear! that isn't nice to say," said Mrs. Bobbsey. "We thought it better to let you sleep."

"Well, I wish I'd seen the fire," said Flossie. "I like to look at something that's bright and shiny."

"Then you'll have a chance to see something like that this afternoon," said Mr. Bobbsey to his little girl.

"Where?" asked all the Bobbsey twins at once, for when their father talked this way Nan and Bert were as eager as Flossie and Freddie.

"How would you all like to go to a theater show this afternoon—to a matinee?" asked Mr. Bobbsey.

"Oh, lovely!" cried Flossie.

"Could Nell and Billy go?" asked Nan, kindly thinking of her little new friends.

"Yes, we'll take the Martin children," Mr. Bobbsey promised.

"And will there be some red fire in the theater show?" Flossie wanted to know.

"I think so," said her father. "It is a fairy play, about Cinderella, and some others like her, and I guess there will be plenty of bright lights and red fire."

"Will there be a fire engine?" asked Freddie. Of course you might have known, without my telling you, that it was Freddie who asked that question. But I thought I'd put his name down to make sure.

"I don't know about there being a fire engine in the play," said Mr. Bobbsey. "I hardly think there will be one. But the play will be very nice, I'm sure."

"I think so, too," said Mrs. Bobbsey. "We'll have a fine time."

"Will there be any cowboys or Indians in it?" Bert asked.

"Well, hardly, I think," his father answered. "But if we don't like the play, after we get there, we can come home," he added, his eyes twinkling.

"Oh, Daddy!" cried all the Bobbsey twins at once. And then, by the way their father smiled, they knew he was only joking.

"Oh, we'll stay," laughed Bert.

"Oh, it's snowing!" cried Freddie as they left the breakfast table and went to sit in the

main parlor of the hotel. "It's snowing, and
we can have sleigh rides."

"If it gets deep enough," put in Bert. "I
guess it won't be very deep here, will it,
Daddy?"

"Well, sometimes there is quite a bit of
snow in Washington," answered Mr. Bobbsey.
"We'll have to wait and see."

"The snow won't keep us from going to
show in the theater; will it?" asked Nan.

"No," her mother said. "Nor to see the show
given there," she added, smiling.

After a visit to the Martins, to tell them of
the treat in store, the tickets were purchased,
the Bobbseys had dinner, and, in due time, the
merry little party was at the theater.

They were shown to their seats, and then the
children looked around, waited eagerly for the
curtain to go up, while Mr. and Mrs. Bobbsey
talked together. More and more people came
in. There were a large number of children,
for it was a play especially for them, though,
of course, lots of "grown-ups" came also.

The musicians entered and took their places
in the funny little place back of a brass rail,

Then came the delicious thrills of the squeaking violins as they were tuned, the tap-tap of the drum, the tinkle of a piano, and the soft, low notes of a flute.

"Oh, it's going to begin soon," whispered Nell to Nan.

"I hope it's a good show," said Bert to his chum Billy, and trying to speak as if he went to a matinee every other day at least.

"Oh, they have pretty good shows here," Billy said.

"Look!" suddenly whispered Nan, pointing to a box at their left. "Look at the Chinese children!"

And, surely enough, into a near-by box came several boys and girls about the age of the Bobbsey twins, and some almost babies, but they were dressed in beautiful blue, golden and red silken garments. And with them came their father, who also wore a silk robe of blue, embroidered with golden birds.

"Who are they—some of the actors in the play?" asked Bert.

"No, that's the Chinese minister and some of his family, and I guess some of their friends," explained Billy. "I've seen them before. They don't often dress up in the same kind of clothes they wear in China, but they did to-day."

"Oh, aren't they cute!" said Nell to Nan.

"Too lovely for anything!" agreed Nan enthusiastically.

Many eyes were on the box, but the Chinese minister and his beautifully dressed children did not seem to mind being looked at. The children were just as much interested in staring about the theater as were the Bobbsey twins, and the Oriental tots probably thought that the other children were even more queer than the American boys and girls thought the Chinese to be.

Having given a good deal of attention to the Chinese children in the box, the Bobbseys looked around the theater at the other little folk in the audience.

"Oh, look at the funny fat boy over there!" cried out Freddie in a loud voice.

"Hush, hush, Freddie!" whispered Nan quickly. "You mustn't talk so loud. Every one will hear you."

"But he is awful fat, isn't he?" insisted Freddie.

"He isn't any fatter than you'll be if you keep on eating so much," remarked Bert.

"Oh, I don't eat any more than I have to," declared the little boy. "When you are really and truly hungry you can't help eating. Nobody can!"

"And you're hungry most all the time," said Bert.

"I'm not at all! I'm hungry only when—when—I'm hungry," was Freddie's reply.

Then the orchestra began to play, and, a little later, the curtain went up and the fairy play began.

I am not going to tell you about it, because you all know the story of Cinderella. There she was, sitting among the ashes of the fire-place, and in came the godmother who made a pumpkin turn into a golden coach, and did all the other things just like the story.

The play was a little different from the story in some books. In one scene a bad fairy sets off a lighted fire cracker under the palace of the princess. And on the stage, when this happened, there was a loud banging noise, just as Bert and Nan had often heard on the Fourth of July.

"Bang!" went the fire cracker.

"Oh!" cried Nell, and she gave a little jump. she was so surprised. And many other were surprised, too, including the little Oriental children. And they were so surprised that the smaller ones burst out crying.

"Oh dear! Oh dear!" they cried, in their own language, of course, and the two smallest hid their faces down in their father's lap and cried salty tears on his beautiful blue robe. But he didn't seem to mind a bit.

He patted the heads of the little, sobbing tots, and every one in the theater looked over toward the box, for the crying of the Chinese children, who were frightened by the bang of the fire cracker, was very loud crying indeed.

CHAPTER XIX

"OH LOOK!"

FOR a time the actors on the stage, taking part in the fairy play, had to stop. They could not go on because the Chinese children were crying so hard. And really it was a strange thing to have happen.

Then Cinderella herself—or at least the young lady who was playing that part—seeing what the matter was, stepped to the front of the stage and said to the Chinese minister:

"Tell your little children there will be no more shooting. They will not be frightened again. I am sorry it happened," and she bowed and kissed her hand to the older boys and girls in the box. They were not frightened as were the smaller ones.

"It is all right. They will be themselves again soon. I thank you," said the Chinese minister, rising and bowing to the actress. He spoke in English, but with a queer little twist to his words, just as we would speak queerly if we tried to talk Chinese.

Then the sobbing of the frightened children gradually ceased, and the play went on. But the Bobbsey twins were almost as much interested in the queer, beautifully dressed foreign children in the box as they were in the play itself. Indeed Flossie and Freddie looked from the stage to the box and from the box back to the stage again so often that their mother said they would have stiff necks. However, they didn't have, which only goes to show that children's necks can stand a great deal of twisting and turning without getting tired.

So the play went on, and very pretty it was. Cinderella tried on the glass slipper. It fitted perfectly, and everything came out all right, and she and the prince lived happily forever after.

"Is that all?" asked Flossie, when the curtain went down for the last time, and the people began getting up to leave.

"That's all," her mother told her. "Didn't you like it?"

"Oh, yes, it was nice," said Flossie. "But they didn't have as much red fire as I wanted to see."

"And they didn't have a single fire engine!" sighed Freddie.

"Too bad!" laughed Bert. "We'll look for a show for you, Freddie, where they have nothing but fire engines!"

But, after all, even without quite enough red fire and not a fire engine on the stage, the play was enjoyed by the Bobbsey twins and their little friends, the Martin children.

"Where are we going?" asked Nan, as they came out of the theater and Mr. Bobbsey led the children toward a big automobile that stood at the curb.

"We are going to the Martins for the evening," answered Daddy Bobbsey. "Mr. Martin sent down his auto for us, so we don't have to go out in the storm."

"It was very kind of him," added Mrs. Bobbsey.

"I like the snow!" cried Freddie. "I'm going to make a snow fort, to-morrow, and a snow man."

"And I'm going to make a little snow doll!" declared Flossie.

"Wait until you see if there's snow enough," advised Bert.

"Will there be much, do you think?" Nan inquired of Nell.

"Well, we don't often have a very heavy fall of snow here," was the answer, "though it sometimes happens. It's snowing hard now."

And so it was. And the weather was getting cold, too, almost as cold as back in Lakeport. But the Bobbseys were used to it. Their eyes were shining and their cheeks were red. Flossie and Freddie tried to catch the drifting snow flakes dancing down from the sky. But there was quite a crowd on the sidewalk coming out of the theater, and every one seemed to get in the way of the little Bobbsey twins, so they did not have much luck catching the white crystals.

Into the big, closed auto they piled, and soon they were rolling along the snow-covered streets of Washington toward the home of Nell and Billy Martin. Mr. and Mrs. Martin would be waiting at their house to greet the Bobb seys. It was dark, now, and the lighted lamps made the snow sparkle like a million diamonds.

"Oh, it's just lovely!" sighed Nan, as she leaned back against the cushions and peered from the window.

"It looks just like a fairy play out there" and Nell pointed to the glittering snow.

"It looks like—like one of those funny Christmas cards that twinkle so!" declared Freddie.

"Oh, it will soon be Christmas, won't it?" exclaimed Flossie, who sat on her mother's lap. "I wonder what I'll get!"

"I want something, too!" cried Freddie. "Oh, won't it be nice at Christmas!"

"Yes, it will soon be here—much sooner than we think," said Mr. Bobbsey.

"Shall we go home for Christmas?" Nan asked.

"Oh, yes," her father told her. "My business here is nearly finished, and we'll go back to Lakeport next week."

"Aren't we going to buy anything to take home—souvenirs I mean?" added Bert. "I promised to bring Sam something."

"And I want to take Dinah a present!" declared Nan.

"Yes, we must do a little shopping for things like that," said Mrs. Bobbsey. "You children will have a chance next week."

And they talked of that, and the things they would buy, until the automobile stopped at the Martin house, when they all went inside.

After supper, or dinner as it is more often called, the children had fun playing games and looking at picture books, while the older folk talked among themselves. Mr. and Mrs. Martin were quite interested in hearing of how the Chinese children cried when the fire cracker went off.

"I have never seen any of the ambassadors or the ministers from the Oriental countries wear their native dress," said Mr. Martin. "But there is no reason why they shouldn't."

"No," said Mr. Bobbsey, "there isn't. If we went to a foreign country we would want to wear the clothes we had always worn at home, and we wouldn't like to be stared at for doing it, either."

The evening passed pleasantly, but at last

Mrs. Bobbsey noticed that Flossie and Freddie were getting sleepy, so she said they would have to go back to the hotel and to bed.

"And I hope the fire engines don't wake us up to-night," said Nan. "I want to sleep."

"I do, too," added her mother.

Nothing happened that night, and in the morning there was enough snow on the ground for the making of a small snow man, at least, and as many snowballs as the children wanted to throw at him. Flossie and Freddie were warmly dressed, and allowed to play out in a little yard in front of the hotel. It was rather a treat for Washington children to have as much snow as they now had, and many were out enjoying it.

Flossie and Freddie played as they did at home, and Bert and Nan, with Nell and Billy Martin, who came over, watched the smaller twins.

"Let's throw snowballs at a target," said Freddie presently. "I'm going to play I'm a soldier and shoot the cannon."

"You haven't any target, Freddie Bobbsey," declared Flossie.

"Yes, I have, too!" answered her twin brother. "Just look here!"

Freddie had espied a small tin can standing in an areaway not far away. He ran to get this, and then set it up on a near-by iron railing.

"There's my target!" he exclaimed; and both he and Flossie began to throw snowballs at it and were in high glee when the can tumbled over.

Thus the fun went on for some time.

After lunch Mrs. Bobbsey said:

"Now, children, if you wish, you may go out and buy some souvenirs. As long as Nell and Billy are here to go with you, I will not have to go, since they know their way about the streets near our hotel. I'm going to give you each a certain sum, and you may spend it in any way you like for souvenirs to take home to Sam, Dinah and your other friends. Now start out and have a good time."

The snow had stopped and the sun was shining, which meant that the white covering would not last long. But it gave a touch of winter to Washington, and the children liked it.

Down the street went the six children, two by two, the four Bobbsey twins and Nell and Billy Martin. Flossie and Freddie walked together, then came Billy and Bert, while Nan walked with Nell.

"Here's a store where they have nice things," said Nell, as they stopped in front of one, the windows of which held all sorts of light and pretty articles, from fans and postcards to vases and pocket knives, some with tiny photographic views of Washington set in the handles.

"Let's go in there and buy something," proposed Bert.

In they trooped, and you may well believe me when I say that the woman who kept this store had a busy half-hour trying to wait on the four Bobbsey twins at once. Nell and Billy did not want to buy anything, but the Bobbseys did.

At last, however, each one had bought something, and then Bert said:

"I know where to go next."

"Where?" asked Nan.

"Around the corner," her brother answered,

as they came out of the souvenir shop. "There's a cheaper place there. I looked in the windows yesterday and saw the prices marked. We haven't got much money left, and we've got to go to a cheap place for the rest of our things."

"All right," agreed Nan, and Bert led the way. The other store, just as he said, was only around the corner, and, as he had told his sister, the windows were filled with many things, some of them marked at prices which were very low.

Suddenly, as Nan was peering in through the glass, she gave a startled cry, and, plucking Bert by the sleeve, exclaimed:

"Oh, look!"

CHAPTER XX

A GREAT BARGAIN

Bert Bobbsey turned to look at his sister Nan. She was staring at something in the jumble of articles in the second-hand shop window, and what she saw seemed to excite Nan.

"What is it? What's the matter?" asked Bert, as Nan, once more, exclaimed:

"Look! Oh, look!"

"Is it a fire?" eagerly asked Freddie, as he wiggled about to get a better view of the window, since Bert and Nan stood so near it he could not see very well. "Is it a fire?"

"Oh, you and your fires!" laughed Nell, as she put her hands lovingly on his shoulders. "Don't you ever think of anything else?"

"Oh, is it a fire?" asked Freddie again.

"No, there isn't any fire," answered Billy, laughing, as his sister Nell was doing, at Freddie's funny ideas.

"But it's something!" insisted Flossie, who had, by this time, wiggled herself to a place beside Freddie, and so near the window that she could flatten her little nose against it.

"What is it you see, Nan?" asked Bert. "If it's more souvenirs I don't believe we can buy any. My money is 'most gone."

"Oh, but we must get these even if we have to go home for more money!" exclaimed Nan. "Look, Bert! Right near those old brass candlesticks. See that sugar bowl and pitcher?"

"I see 'em!" answered Bert.

"Don't you know whose they are?" rapidly whispered Nan. "Look at the way they're painted? And see! On the bottom of the sugar bowl is a blue lion! I can't see the letters 'J. W.' but they must be there. Oh, Bert! don't you know what this means? Can't you see? Those are Miss Pompret's missing dishes that she told us she'd give a hundred dollars to get back! And oh, Bert! we've got to go in there and buy that sugar bowl and cream pitcher, and we can take 'em back to Miss Pompret at Lakeport, and she'll give us a hundred dollars, and—and——"

But Nan was so excited and out of breath that she could not say another word. She could just manage to hold Bert's sleeve and point at the window of the second-hand shop.

At last Bert "woke up," as he said afterward. His eyes opened wider, and he stared with all his might at what Nan was pointing toward. There, surely enough, among some old candlesticks, a pair of andirons, a bellows for blowing a fire, was a sugar bowl and cream pitcher. And it needed only a glance to make Bert feel sure that the two pieces of china were decorated just as were Miss Pompret's.

But there was something more than this. The sugar bowl was turned over so that the bottom part was toward the street. And on the bottom, plainly to be seen, was a circle of gold. Inside the circle was a picture of some animal in blue, and Nan, at least, felt sure it was a blue lion. As she had said, no letters could be seen, but they might be there.

"Don't you see, Bert?" asked Nan, as her brother waited several seconds before speaking. "Don't you see that those are Miss Pompret's dishes?"

"Well," admitted the Bobbsey lad, "they look like 'em."

"They surely are!" declared Nan. "Oh, I'm so excited! Let's go right in and buy them. Then we'll get a hundred dollars!"

She darted away from Bert's side, and was about to move toward the door of the shop when Billy caught her by the coat sleeve.

"Wait a minute, Nan," he said.

"What for?" she asked.

"Until Bert and I talk this over," went on Billy, who, though he was not much older than Nan, seemed to be, perhaps because he had lived in a large city all his life. "You don't want to rush in and buy those dishes so quick."

"Why not?" demanded Nan. "If I don't get 'em somebody else may, and you know Miss Pompret offered a reward of a hundred dollars. These are the two pieces missing from her set. Her set is 'broken,' as she calls it, if she doesn't have this sugar bowl and pitcher."

"Yes, I remember your telling me about Miss Pompret's reward," said Billy. "But you'd better go a bit slow."

"Maybe somebody else'll buy 'em!" exclaimed Nan.

"Oh, I don't believe they will," said Nell. "This is a quiet street, and this shop doesn't do much business. We only come here once in a while because some things are cheaper. We never bought any second-hand things."

"There's nobody coming down the street now," observed Bert, who was beginning to agree with Billy in the matter. "If we see any one going in that we think will buy the dishes, we can hurry in ahead of 'em. We'll stand here and talk a minute. What is it you want to say, Billy?"

"Well, it's like this," went on the Washington boy. "I know these second-hand men. If they think you want a thing they'll charge you a lot of money for it. But if they think you don't want it very much they will let you have it cheap. I know, 'cause a fellow and I wanted to get a baseball glove in here one day. It was a second-hand one, but good. The fellow I was with knew just how to do it.

"He went in, and asked the price of a lot of things, and said they were all too high. Then

he asked the price of the glove, just as if he
didn't care much whether he got it or not. The
man said it was a dollar, but when Jimmie—
the boy who was with me—said he only had
eighty cents, the man let him have the glove
for that."

"Oh, I see what you mean!" cried Nan.
"You mean we must try to get a bargain."

"Yes," said Billy. "Otherwise, if you go
in and want to buy those dishes first thing, the
man may want five dollars for 'em."

"Oh, we haven't that much money!" cried
Nan, much surprised.

"That's why I say we must go slow," said
Billy. "Now you leave this to me and Bert."

"I think it would be a good idea," declared
Nell.

"All right! I will," agreed Nan. "But, oh,
I do hope we can get those dishes for Miss
Pompret."

"And I hope we can get the reward of a
hundred dollars," murmured Bert.

"I only hope they're the right dishes," said
Billy.

"Oh, I'm sure they are," declared Nan,

"They have the blue lion on and everything. And if they have the letters 'J. W.' on, then we'll know for sure. Let's go in and see."

"We've got to go slow," declared Billy. "Mustn't be too fast. Let Bert and me go ahead."

"I want to come in, too!" declared Freddie. "I want to buy a whistle. Do they have whistles in here?"

"I guess so," answered Bert. "It will be a good thing to go in and ask for, anyhow."

"Sort of excuse for going in," suggested Nell.

"Do they have ice cream cones?" asked Flossie. "I want something to eat."

"I don't believe they have anything to eat in here," said Nell. "But we can get that later, Flossie. Now you and Freddie be nice when we go in, and after we come out I'll get you some ice cream."

"I'll be good!" promised Flossie.

"So'll I," agreed Freddie. "But I want a whistle, and if they have a little fire engine I want that."

"You don't want much!" laughed Bert.

"Well, let's go in!" suggested Billy.

So, with the two boys in the lead, followed by Nell and Nan and Flossie and Freddie, the children entered the second-hand and souvenir store.

A bell on the door rang with a loud clang as Billy opened it, and when the children stepped inside the shop an old man with a black, curly beard and long black hair that seemed as if it had never been combed, came out from a back room.

"What you want to buy, little childrens?" he asked. "I got a lot of nice things, cheap! Very cheap!"

"Well, if you've got something very cheap we might buy it," answered Billy, with as nearly a grown-up manner as he could assume. "But we haven't much money."

"Ha! Ha! That's what they all say!" exclaimed the old man. "But everybody has more money that what I has. I'm very poor. I don't hardly make a living I sell things so cheap. What you want to buy, little childrens?"

"Have you got any whistles or fire engines?" burst out Freddie, unable to wait any longer.

"Whistles? Lots of 'em!" exclaimed the man. "Here is a finest whistle what ever was. Listen to it!"

He took one from the show case and blew into it. Not a sound came out.

"Ach! I guess that one is damaged," he said. "But I got other ones. Here! Listen to this!"

The next one blew loud and shrill.

"I want that!" cried Freddie.

"Ten cents!" said the man, holding it out to the little boy.

"What?" cried Billy. "Why, I can buy those whistles for five cents anywhere in Washington! Ten cents? I guess not!"

"Oh, well, take it for seven cents then," said the man. "What I care if I die poor. Take it for seven cents!"

"No, sir!" exclaimed Billy firmly. "Five cents is all they cost, and this is an old one."

"Oh, well. Take is for five then. What I care if you cheats a poor old man? Such a boy as you are! Take it for five cents!" and he handed the whistle to Freddie. But before he could take it Nan said, gently:

"I think it would be better for him to have a fresh one from the box. That is all dusty."

The truth was she did not want Freddie to take a whistle the old man had blown into.

"Oh, well, I gives you a fresh one," he said, and he took a new and shining one from the box. Freddie blew it, making a shrill sound.

"What else you want to buy, little childrens?" asked the old man. "I sell everythings cheap—everythings!"

"Ask how much the dishes are," whispered Nan to Billy. But he shook his head, and looked around the shop. He looked everywhere but at the window where the dishes were.

"Any sailboats?" asked Billy, as if that was all he had come in to inquire about.

"Sailboats?" cried the man. "Sailboats?"

"Yes, toy sailboats."

"No, I haven't got any of them, but I got a nice football. Here I show you!"

"I don't want a football. You can't play football when the snow is on the ground!" exclaimed Bert, as the man started toward some shelves on the other side of the room.

"I want a doll," whispered Flossie. "Just a little doll."

"A doll!" exclaimed the man. "Sure I gots a fine lot of dolls. See!"

Quickly he held out a large one with very blue eyes and hair just like Flossie's.

"Only a dollar seventy-five," he said. "Very cheap!"

"Oh, that's too much!" exclaimed Nan. "We haven't that much money. She wants only a little ten-cent doll."

"Oh, well, I have them kinds too!" said the man, in disappointed tones. "Here you are!"

He held out one that did not appear to be very nice.

"You can get those for five cents in the other stores," whispered Nell.

"Better take it," said her brother. "Then I'll ask about the dishes."

"Yes, we'll take it," agreed Nan.

So Flossie was given her doll, and, even though it might have been only five cents somewhere else, she liked it just as well.

"What else you wants to buy, childrens?" asked the old man. "I got lots more things so cheap—oh, so very cheap!"

Billy and Bert strolled over to the window. They looked down in. Nan crowded to their side. She felt sure, now, that the two pieces of china were the very ones Miss Pompret wanted. If they could only get that sugar bowl and pitcher!

"I wish you had a sailboat!" murmured Billy, as if that was all he cared about. Then, turning to Nan he asked: "Would you like that sugar bowl and pitcher?"

"Oh, yes, I think I would!" she exclaimed, trying not to make her voice seem too eager.

"You might have a play party with them," Billy went on. If Miss Pompret could have heard him then I feel sure she would have fainted, or had what Dinah would call "a cat in a fit."

"You want those dishes?" asked the old man, as he reached over and lifted the sugar bowl and pitcher from his window. "Ach! them is a great bargain. I let you have them cheap. And see, not a chip or a crack on 'em

Good china, too! Very valuable, but they is all I have left. I sells 'em cheap."

Bert took the sugar bowl and looked closely at it, while Nan took the pitcher. The children felt sure these were the same pieces that would fill out Miss Pompret's set.

"Look at the mark on the bottom," whispered Nan to Bert, as the storekeeper hurried to the other side of the room to rescue a pile of chairs which Freddie seemed bent on pulling down. "Is the blue lion there?"

"Yes," answered Bert, "it is."

"And the letters 'J. W.'?"

"Yes," Bert replied. "But, somehow, it doesn't look like the one on Miss Pompret's plates."

"Oh, I'm sure it's the same one!" insisted Nan. "We've found the missing pieces, Bert, and we'll get——"

"Hush!" cautioned Billy, for the old man was coming back.

"You want to buy them?" he asked. "I sell cheap. It's a great bargain."

"Where did they come from?" asked Bert.

"Come from? How shoulds I know. Maybe I get 'em at a fire sale, or maybe all the other dishes in that set get broken, and these all what are left. Somebody bring 'em in, and I buys 'em, or my wife she buys 'em. How can I tells so long ago?"

"Oh, well, maybe we might take 'em for the girls to have a play party with their own set of dishes," went on Billy. "But I wish you had a toy ship. How much for these dishes— this sugar bowl and pitcher?"

"How much? Oh, I let you have these very cheap. They is worth five dollars—very rare china—very thin but hard to break. These is a good bargain—a great bargain. You shall have them for—two dollars!"

CHAPTER XXI

JUST SUPPOSE

NAN BOBBSEY gave gasp, just as if she had fallen into a bath tub full of cold water. Bert quickly glanced at his friend Billy. Nell had hurried over to the other side of the room to stop Flossie from pulling a pile of dusty magazines from a shelf down on top of herself. Billy seemed to be the only one who was not excited.

"Two dollars?" he repeated. "That's a lot of money."

"What? A lot of money for rich childrens? Ha! Ha! That's only a little moneys!" laughed the man, rubbing his hands.

"We aren't rich," said Bert. "And I don't believe we have two dollars." He was pretty sure he and Nan had not that much, at any rate.

"How much you got?" asked the man

eagerly. "Maybe I let you have these dishes cheaper, but they's worth more as two dollars. How much you all got?"

"How much have you?" asked Billy of Bert. Bert pulled some change from his pocket. The two boys counted it.

"Eighty-seven cents," announced Bert, when they had counted it twice.

"Oh, that isn't half enough!" cried the old man.

"I have some money," announced Nan, bringing out her little purse.

"How much?" asked the man. That seemed to be all he could think about.

Nan and Nell counted the change. It amounted to thirty-two cents.

"How much is thirty-two and eighty-seven?" asked Nell.

Bert and Billy figured it on a piece of paper.

"A dollar and twenty-nine cents," announced Bert.

"No, it's only a dollar and nineteen," declared Billy, who was a little better at figures than was his chum.

"How much?" asked the old man, for the

children had done their counting on the other
side of the room, and in whispers.

"A dollar and nineteen cents!" announced
Billy.

"Oh, I couldn't let you have these dishes
for that," said the old man, and he seemed
about to take them from the counter where
they had been put, to place them back in the
window.

"Wait a minute," said Billy. "These dishes
are worth only a dollar, but I have fifteen cents
I can lend you, Bert. That will make a dollar
and thirty-four cents. That's all we have and
if you don't want to sell the dishes for that, we
can go and get 'em somewhere else."

Nan was about to gasp out: "Oh!" but a
look from Billy stopped her. She saw what he
was trying to do.

"A dollar thirty-four—that's all the moneys
you got?" asked the old man.

"Every cent we're going to give!" declared
Billy firmly. "If you'll sell the play dishes
for that all right. If you won't——"

He seemed about to leave.

"Oh, well, what I cares if I die in the poorhouse?" asked the old man. "Here! Take 'em. But I am losing money. Those is valuable dishes. If I had more I could sell 'em for ten dollars maybe. But as they is all I got take 'em for a dollar and thirty-four. You couldn't make it a dollar thirty-five, could you?"

"No," said Bert decidedly, "we couldn't!"

"Oh, dear!" sighed the old man. "Take 'em, then."

"They're awfully dusty," complained Nell, as she looked at the sugar bowl and pitcher.

"That's 'cause they're so old and valuable, my dear," snarled the old man. "But my wife she dust them off for you, and I wrap them up, though I ought to charge you a penny for a sheet of paper. But what I care if I dies in the poorhouse."

"Are you goin' there soon?" asked Flossie. "We've got a poorhouse at Lakeport, and it's awful nice."

"Oh, well, little one, maybe I don't go there just yet," said the man who spoke wrong words sometimes. "Here, Mina!" he called, and a woman, almost as old as he, came from the

back room. "Wipe off the dust. I have sold
the old dishes—the valuable old dishes."

"Ah, such a bargain as they got!" murmured
the old woman. "Them is valuable china.
Such a bargains!"

"Where did you get them?" asked Nan, as
the dishes were being wrapped and the old
man was counting over the nickles, dimes and
pennies of the children's money.

"Where I get them? Of how should I
know? Maybe they come in by somebody
what sell them for money. Maybe we buy
them in some old house like Washington's. It
is long ago. We have had them in the shop
a long time, but the older they are the better
they get. They is all the better for being old
—a better bargain, my dear!" and the old
woman smiled, showing a mouth from which
many teeth were missing.

"Well, come on," said Billy, when the dishes
had been wrapped and given to Bert, who carried them carefully. "But I wish you had some
sailboats," he said to the old man, as if that
was all they had come in to buy.

"I have some next week," answered the old

man. "Comes around then and have a big bargains in a sailsboats."

"Maybe I will," agreed Billy.

Out of the shop walked the Bobbsey twins and their chums, the Martin children of Washington. And the hearts of Bert and Nan, at least, were beating quickly with excitement and hope. As for Flossie, she was holding her doll, and Freddie was blowing his whistle.

"I'm a regular fire engine now," declared Freddie. "Don't you hear how the engine is blowing the whistle?"

"You'll have everybody looking at you, Freddie Bobbsey!" exclaimed Flossie. "Nan, do make him stop his noise."

"Oh, let him blow his whistle if he wants to," said Bert. "It isn't hurting anybody."

"I know what I'm going to do when I get home," said Flossie. "I'm going to put a brand new dress on this doll, and give her a new hat, too."

"That will be nice," said Nan.

At that moment they had to cross at a street corner which was much crowded. There was a policeman there to regulate the coming and going of the people and carriages and automobiles, and when he blew his whistle the traffic would go up and down one street, and then when he blew his whistle again it would go up and down the other.

The policeman had just blown on his whistle, and the traffic was going past the Bobbsey twins when Freddie gave a sudden loud blow. Immediately some of the carriages and automobiles going in one direction stopped short and the others commenced to go the other way.

"For gracious sake, Freddie! see what you have done," gasped Bert.

The traffic policeman who stood in the middle of the two streets looked very much surprised. Then he saw it was Freddie who had blown the whistle, and he shook his finger at the little boy in warning.

"He wants you to stop," said Nan, and made Freddie put the whistle in his pocket for the time being.

Then the Bobbseys and their friends hurried on their way.

"I'll give you the fifteen cents as soon as we get back to the hotel, Billy," said Bert.

"Oh, that's all right," his chum answered. "I'm in no hurry. Do you think we paid too much for the dishes?"

"Oh, no!" exclaimed Nan. "I'd have given the two dollars if I'd had it. Why, Miss Pompret will give us a hundred dollars for these two pieces."

"That's fifty dollars apiece!" exclaimed Nell. "It doesn't seem that they could be worth that."

"Oh, but she wants them to make up her set," said Bert. "Just these two pieces are missing. I wonder how they came to be in that second-hand store?"

"Maybe the tramp who took them years ago brought them here and sold them," suggested Nan. "But I don't suppose we'll ever really find out."

Eager and excited, the Bobbsey twins and their friends walked back toward the hotel.

"Won't mother and father be surprised when they find we have the Pompret china?" asked Nan of her brother,

"Yes," he answered, "I guess they will. But, oh, Nan! Just suppose!"

"Suppose what?" she asked, for Bert seemed worried over something.

"Suppose these aren't the right dishes, after all? S'posin' these aren't the ones Miss Pompret wants?"

CHAPTER XXII

HAPPY DAYS

NAN BOBBSEY was so surprised by what Bert said that she stood still in the street and looked at her brother. Then she looked at the precious package he was carrying.

"Bert Bobbsey!" she exclaimed, "these *must* be the same as Miss Pompret's! Why they have the blue lion on, and the circle of gold, and the letters 'J. W.' and—and everything!"

"Yes, I saw that, too," agreed Bert. "But still they might not be the same dishes."

"Oh, dear!" sighed Nan. "And we paid all that money, too!"

"Oh, I guess they must be the same," put in Nell. "Anyhow, you can take 'em to the hotel and ask your mother."

"Yes, mother might know," agreed Nan.

"And if she says those dishes aren't the ones you want, why we can take 'em back and

231

the man will give us our money," said Billy.

"Oh, he'd never do that!" declared Bert.

"Well, we can ask him," went on the Washington lad.

"Maybe the dishes are Miss Pompret's, after all," said Bert. "I was just s'posin'. And if they aren't, why we can give 'em to Dinah for souvenirs. I was going to get her something anyhow."

"But they cost a lot of money," objected Nan.

"Well, Dinah is awful good to us," said Bert. "And she'd like these dishes if they aren't Miss Pompret's."

"But I do hope they are," sighed Nan, "Think of a whole hundred dollars!"

"It would scare me to get all that money," said Nell. "Oh, I do hope they are the right sugar bowl and pitcher!"

Back to the hotel hurried the Bobbsey twins. Flossie and Freddie, happy with their toys— the doll and the whistle—did not care much one way or the other about the dishes and the reward. But Bert and Nan were very much excited.

"Well, you've been gone rather a long time buying souvenirs," said Mrs. Bobbsey, when the twins and the Martin children came in.

"And oh, Mother, we've had the most wonderful time!" burst out Nan. "We've found Miss Pompret's missing china dishes—the two she has wanted so long—the ones the tramp took and she's going to give a reward of a hundred dollars for, you know—and—and——"

"Yes, and I know you're excited!" exclaimed Mrs. Bobbsey. "Now cool down and tell me all about it."

"And here are the dishes," added Bert, as he set the precious bundle down on the table. "Look at 'em, Mother, and see if they are the ones like Miss Pompret's set. You saw her dishes, didn't you?"

"Yes, but I am not sure I would know them again."

"I owe Billy fifteen cents," went on Bert, as he unwrapped the dishes. "We didn't have money enough. The man wanted two dollars, but Billy got him down to a dollar and thirty-four cents."

"Billy is quite a little bargainer," said Mrs. Bobbsey, with a smile. "And now to look at the dishes."

She carefully examined the sugar bowl and cream pitcher. There was no doubt about the blue lion in the circle of gold being stamped on the bottom of each piece. There were also the initials "J. W." which might stand for Jonathan Waredon, the man who made such rare china.

"Well, I should say that these pieces were just like those in Miss Pompret's set," said Mrs. Bobbsey, after a pause. "But whether they are exactly the same or not, I can't tell. She would have to look at them herself."

"I wish we could hurry home and show them to her," sighed Nan.

"So do I," said Bert. "I want to get that hundred dollars."

"Well, we'll be going back to Lakeport in a few days now," said his mother. "Our stay in Washington is nearly over."

"Oh, dear!" sighed Nell. "I wish you could stay longer."

"So do I," added her brother Billy.

Bert gave Billy back the borrowed fifteen cents, and when Mr. Bobbsey, having been out on lumber business, came home, he, too, said he thought the pieces belonged to Miss Pompret's set of rare china.

"But there is only one sure way to tell," the twins' father said. "Miss Pompret must see them herself."

The few remaining days the Bobbsey twins spent in Washington were filled with good times. They were nicely entertained by the Martins, and went on many excursions to places of interest. But, all the while, Bert and Nan, at least, were thinking of the sugar bowl and pitcher, and the hundred dollars reward Miss Pompret had promised.

"I do hope we don't have to give the dishes to Dinah for souvenirs," said Nan to Bert.

"I hope so, too," he agreed. "Anyhow, I bought Dinah a red handkerchief with a yellow border and a green center. She likes bright colors."

"I bought her something, too, and for Sam I got something he can hang on his watch chain," said Nan. "So if we have to give

Dinah the dishes, too, she'll have a lot of souvenirs."

At last the day came when the Bobbseys must leave Washington for Lakeport. Goodbyes were said to the Martins, and they promised to visit the Bobbseys at Lakeport some time. Mr. Bobbsey finished his lumber business, and then with trunks and valises packed and locked, and with the precious dishes put carefully in the middle of a satchel which Bert insisted on carrying, the homeward trip was begun.

Not very much happened on it, except that once Bert forgot the valise with the dishes in it, having left it in a car, but he thought of it in time and ran back to get it just before the train was about to start away with it. After that he was more careful.

"Well, honey lambs! I suah is glad to see yo' all back!" cried Dinah, as she welcomed the Bobbsey twins at their own door. "Come right in, I'se got lots fo' yo' all to eat! Come in, honey lambs! How am mah little fat fairy and' mah little fireman?"

"Oh, we're fine, Dinah!" said Freddie,

"And I saw a real fire and I pulled the fire bell on the boat an'—an'—an'—everything!"

"Bress yo' heart, honey lamb! I guess yo' did!" laughed Dinah.

"And I got a little doll and my hat blew off the steeple!" cried Flossie.

"Lan' sakes! Do tell!" cried Dinah.

"And we found Miss Pompret's dishes!" broke in Nan.

"And we're going to get the hundred dollars reward," added Bert. " 'Cept, of course, if they aren't the right ones you can have 'em for souvenirs, Dinah."

"Bress yo' heart, honey lamb! Dinah's got all she wants when yo' all come back. Now I go an' git somethin' to eat!"

The children—at least Nan and Bert—were so eager to have Miss Pompret see the two dishes that they hardly ate any of the good things Dinah provided. They wanted to go at once and call on the dear, old-fashioned lady, but their father and mother made them wait.

At last, however, when they had all rested a bit, Mr. Bobbsey took Nan and Bert with him and went to call on Miss Pompret. The dishes, carefully washed by Mrs. Bobbsey, were carried along, wrapped in soft paper.

"Oh, I am glad to see my little friends again," said Miss Pompret, as she greeted Nan and Bert. "Did you have a nice time in Washington?"

"Yes'm," answered Bert. "And we brought you——"

"We found your missing sugar bowl and pitcher!" broke in Nan. "Anyhow, we hope they're yours, and we paid the old man a dollar and thirty-four cents and——"

"You—you found my sugar bowl and pitcher!" exclaimed Miss Pompret, and Mr. Bobbsey said, afterward, that she turned a little pale. "Really do you mean it—after all these years?"

"Well, they look like your dishes," said Mr. Bobbsey. "The children saw them in a second-hand store window, and went in and bought them. I hope, for your sake, they are the right pieces."

"I can soon tell," said the old lady. "There is not another set like the ancient Pompret china in this country. Oh, I am so anxious!"

Her thin, white hands, themselves almost like china, trembled as she unwrapped the pieces. And then, as she saw them, she gave a cry of joy and exclaimed:

"Yes! They are the very same! Those are the two pieces missing from my set! Now it is complete! Oh, how thankful I am that I have the Pompret cnina set together again! Oh, thank you, children, thank you!" and she threw her arms about Nan and kissed her, while she shook hands with Bert, much to that young boy's relief. He hated being kissed.

"Are you sure these are the two pieces from your set?" asked Mr. Bobbsey.

"Positive," answered Miss Pompret. "See! Here is the blue lion in the circle of gold, and initials 'J. W.' There can be no mistake. And now how did you find them?"

Bert and Nan told, and related how Billy had bargained for the two pieces. They all wondered how the second-hand man had come by them, but they never found out.

Miss Pompret carefully placed the sugar bowl and pitcher in the glass-doored closet with her other pieces. She looked at them for several seconds. They matched perfectly.

"Now, once more, after many years, my precious set of china is together again," she murmured.

She went over to a desk and began to write. A little later she handed a slip of blue paper to Mr. Bobbsey.

"What is this?" he asked.

"A check for one hundred dollars," answered Miss Pompret. "It is the reward I promised for the finding of my china. I have made the check out to you, Mr. Bobbsey. You can get the money and give half to Nan and half to Bert."

Mr. Bobbsey slowly shook his head. Then he handed the blue check back to Miss Pompret.

"Their mother and I couldn't think of letting the children take the hundred dollars just for having discovered your dishes, Miss Pompret," he said. "I thank you very much, but Nan and Bert would not want it, themselves," he went on. "They really did not earn the money. It was just good luck; and so, I'm sure, they would rather the money would go to the Red Cross. Wouldn't you?" he asked Nan and Bert.

For a moment only did they hesitate. Then with a sigh, which she tried hard to keep back, Nan said:

"Oh, yes. It wouldn't be right to take a hundred dollars just for two dishes."

"No," agreed Bert, "it wouldn't. Please give the money to the Red Cross."

Miss Pompret looked from the children to their father, then to the china in the closet and next at the check in her white, thin hand.

"Very well," said the old lady. "Since you wish it, I'll give the hundred dollars to the Red Cross; and very glad I am to do it, Mr. Bobbsey. I would gladly have paid even more to get back my sugar bowl and pitcher."

"It would hardly be right for the children to have so much money," he said. "The Red Cross needs it for poor and starving children in other lands."

"Very well," answered Miss Pompret. "But at least let me give them back the dollar and thirty-four cents they spent to get the dishes.

That was their own spending money, I presume."

"Yes," said Mr. Bobbsey, "it was. And I don't mind if you give that back."

So Nan and Bert did not really lose anything, and soon the disappointed feeling about not getting the reward wore off. They were glad it was to go to the Red Cross.

And the next morning, when they awakened to find the ground a foot deep in snow, their joy knew no bounds. They forgot all about rewards, china dishes, and even Washington

"Now for some coasting!" cried Bert.

"And snow men!" added Freddie.

"And I'm going to make a snow house for my Washington doll!" cried Flossie.

"Oh, I love snow!" ejaculated Nan. "It's lovely to have it come so near Christmas!"

"That's so!" exclaimed Bert. "It soon will be Christmas! Now let's go out and have some fun in the snow!"

And they did, rolling and tumbling about, making snow men and houses, and coasting on their sleds.

Miss Pompret wrote Mr. Bobbsey a letter.

stating that she had sent a check for one hundred dollars to the Red Cross in the names of Bert and Nan Bobbsey.

"That was certainly very nice of her," said Mrs. Bobbsey, when her husband read this letter to her.

"Well, Miss Pompret is a very nice lady," answered Mr. Bobbsey. "I am very glad that the children got those dishes back for her."

In the next story, "The Bobbsey Twins in the Great West," the children have a chance to do more good deeds.

Slowly the snow flakes drifted down, another storm following the first. It was the night before Christmas.

"I wonder what we'll get?" murmured Nan as she and Bert went up to their rooms.

"I hope I get a pair of shoe-hockeys," he said.

"And I want a fur coat," said Nan.

And when Christmas morning dawned, with the sun shining on the new, sparkling snow, it also shone on the piles of presents for the Bobbsey twins.

There were a number for each one, and, in

a separate place on the table were two large packages. One was marked for Nan and the other for Bert, and each bore the words: "From Miss Alicia Pompret, to the little friends who restored my missing china."

"Oh, mine's a fur coat!" cried Nan, as she opened her package. "A fur coat and story books!"

"And mine's shoe-hockeys—the best ever!" shouted Bert. "And an air rifle and books too!"

And so their dreams came true, and it was the happiest Christmas they ever remembered. And Miss Pompret was happy too.

THE END.